Still Got Joy

Someday, the one you gave away,

will be the only one you're wishing for...

J'sat Necolle

A NOVEL

ISBN-10: 0996123407
ISBN-13: 978-0-9961234-0-2

DEDICATION

Some people wait a lifetime but still never find,
"the one" that motivates, inspires and completes them.
I gave life to mine.

For Tasj

My One. My Only.

STILL GOT JOY

 BOOKS

A division of Ana Productions, Inc.
335 Nelson St. Atlanta, GA 30313

 BOOKS and colophon are trademarks of Ana Productions, Inc.

For information about special discounts for bulk purchases, please contact Ana Productions Special Sales at 678-206-7457 or INFO@ANAPRODUCTIONS.ORG

The Ana Productions speakers bureau can bring authors to your live event. For more
Information or to book an event, contact the Ana Productions Speakers Bureau at 678-206-7457 or visit our website at anaproductions.org

Cover design by Za'Tasja Baker
Manufactured in the United States of America

ISBN-10: 0996123407
ISBN-13: 978-0-9961234-0-2

J'Sat Necolle

NIKKI 1

"DAMN!" I screamed, while pounding my hand on the steering wheel of my less than fabulous ride, my trusty 1996 Honda Accord. Here it is...HOTLANTA, Memorial Day weekend and the city is buzzing with people from all over enjoying the festivities of the "A." We've got a Caribbean Festival down at Morris Brown, The Renaissance Festival over off MLK and a Jazz festival down in West End somewhere. Peachtree is still jumping from the parades held earlier today and I know for a fact Piedmont Park is packed to the damn walls with my Judies from the LGBT click, and what the am I doing...riding around in this hot ass car, in this hot ass city, by my damn self...hot as hell, at that so-called man of mine. Whoever said, "Having a piece of man is better than having no man at all," was telling a damn lie! Having a piece of man is just like having a piece of mind, not worth a crap cause the shit just don't function right most of the time.

If people only knew what goes through my head sometimes, I would've been locked away in an insane asylum a long time ago. Right about now, a 4X4 cell at Central State Mental Hospital ain't looking half bad. Humph, at least I wouldn't be lonely; and as fine as I am, I could probably get some quality time with a damn orderly or something. Instead, when people look at me, they think I got my shit together. Humph, they couldn't be further from the truth. True, I have a great job as Vice–President of Marketing at a global software company but hell, the MBA required to hold such a prestigious position did not come cheap. I got more student loans than all get out, so that's where half my money goes. True, I have one of the finest brothas in the "A", but that ain't worth jack when he prefers to spend all his time with his tired ass homeboys, tricking off down at Magic City. True, most women would sign-up for an all-day appointment with Dr. Kevorkian for an ass and waist like mine. What women are paying good money for nowadays, trying to look like Khloe, Kourtney and that other whore, that put her family on the map by making a sex tape, I was blessed with naturally! Instead of having to run over to The Virgin Hair Depot off Moreland to cop some trick's from Indonesia hair to sew into my scalp, I simply wash mine and go. Thanks to the fact, as my mama used to say, "I got Indian in my family." KMSL...when I think about that dumb shit my mama used to say, I just shake my head..."Indian, what damn Indian? You meant to say, slave owner. You got "Mas'er" in your damn family, cause that's where this silky hair and this high-yellow skin came from.

I was in the 5th grade when I first really started learning about slavery. The first book I read on the subject was the Autobiography of Fredrick Douglas, then the Autobiography of Harriet Tubman and once my studies with the history of slavery led me to the great Madam C.J. Walker's memoir... I knew something in the water wasn't right. Or, should I say, something in the water was "white"! One look in the mirror at my rich, creamy, olive complexion; long, silky, sandy hair and this long, straight nose, and I knew then, somewhere down the line my family lineage had been defiled by some nigga hating, pussy loving, son of a bitch that thought it was his God given right to first, own another human being, and secondly, to take a woman's body without her consent and lastly, to sew seeds that he would be too embarrassed to own up to as his own! After that realization, every time I used to hear my mom brag to her clients as she pressed their hair out with that hot, straightening comb, that her and her baby "got good hair," I wanted to scream, "Shut the hell up, you idiot! Somebody got raped and tortured for this so called "good hair"...what the hell are you bragging about!" But needless to say, high-yellow or not, my mama was a real black woman, and was raised by an even "realer" black woman and I was not about to come out my neck side-ways and get the mess smacked out of me! So, until this very day, I rage in silence, rolling my eyes to the back of my head, every time I hear her say that ignorant shit, talking about some, "we got Indian in our family!" Woman, please!

"Nikki, are you listening to me?" "Say something, damnit," I heard Steven yell into my earpiece. Oh, snap! I jerked my head back to attention. Here I was, pulling into my driveway and for the life of me, I can't even remember driving here. The last thing I remember was this selfish bastard on the other end of my phone telling me when he gets off work, he was going to chill with his boys for a minute.

"Oh, I'm listening to you but I ain't heard shit yet!" Snapping my cell shut, I turned Mariah Carey's; "*I Still Believe*" back up on my I-Pop Shuffle, because of course "Susie"(my trusty 1996 Honda Accord) doesn't have a cd player. As I listen to Mariah's heart wrenching trilogy about how she still believes that her and her ex will be back together again because she believes in true love and true love never ends, my mind drifts back to Kevin, my first love. He was just like the cliché'... tall, dark and handsome...just like I like them. He wasn't really a smooth talker, or as the young folks say, he didn't have swag, but it was just something about him. He always knew the right thing to say, he always made me laugh and he was a good listener but more than anything, he loved him some Nikki.

Just as thoughts of Kevin's lovemaking were about to explode inside my head, I heard the sound of Jagged Edge's hit classic; "*Gotta Be*" escape from my cell phone. Ignoring Steven's trifling ass, I turned the phone completely off. "Fuck you," I said to the silenced phone, looked into my rearview mirror and backed out of my just entered driveway. It's Saturday, I'm beautiful, smart and lonely and I'll be monkey's butt if I keep sitting up in this house by my self, waiting for his worthless self to realize he's got a queen at home.

I turned my cell back on, just to see. I had three voice mail messages and two texts from his tired ass. Oh well. I called my girl, Shayla. "Hey, chick, what's up with ya?" She answered cheerfully.

"Damn, what you so happy about? " I asked dryly.

"Hon-ney, why must your girl need a reason to be happy besides the fact that God woke me up this morning; He started me on my way and I just saved money by switching to Geico. Child, I am blessed and highly favored!" She spouted cheerfully into the receiver. After an awkward silence, she finally noticed it wasn't like me not to return a laugh at her unsolicited humor, she asked, "What's wrong with you or do I even have to ask?" She added flatly.

"Humph, Trick, spare me the saved, sanctified and filled with the Holy Ghost act, I know you...you must've got you some last night?"

" Girl, Yasssssssss!" "And this morning, and I might go back and jump on that "d" right now, since you mentioned it!" She laughed.

Rolling my eyes and sucking my teeth, I just hung up on her ass. That's my girl and all, but I can't help but hate just a little. I can't understand how she can manage to get every man she dates to fall head over hills in love with her. I tell her all the time, you must have some darn good coochie or you give one helluva blow job, cause you have these dudes walking around here like little pink panty wearing sorority sisters. What on earth am I doing wrong? I can hear her in my head now singing, "*I-N-D-E-P-E-N-D-E-N-T, do you know what that mean...you got your own house, you got your own car, two jobs, work hard, you a bad broad...*" then screaming, "But ho, you lonely as hell!"

With Shayla's out of tune voice, ringing in my ears, I made a U-turn at the end of my street and drove my pathetic ass back up the hill to my house. Once inside, I instinctively threw my gym bag in the closet, took off my running shoes so I could feel the plush carpet through my freshly manicured toes, headed straight for the freezer and grabbed the half-eaten carton of my favorite, Pecan Praline Ice cream. Grabbing a spoon, I headed straight for the stairs. When I entered my bedroom, with a spoonful of ice cream in my mouth, the loneliness slapped me in the face like a ton of bricks. Instinctively, I lay across the bed, ate the rest of my ice cream and cried myself to sleep. Again...

MAYA 2

"HELLO" I mumbled into the receiver of my cell, barely able to open my eyes. Glancing over at the alarm clock sitting on my night stand, 5:30am, what the hell...

"Babe, " Steven drooled, "Let me in, babe. Stop trippin."

"Where the hell is your key and whose phone are you calling me from?"

Letting out a loud burp, he announces, "Babe, I was too drunk to drive, I lost my wallet and my cell. I'm in a taxi, this is the driver's cell."

"Humph, right, and I'm Boo Boo The Fool," I mumbled, taking my own sweet time getting up from my warm bed, where it seemed like I had just closed my eyes. In between Vesta Williams', "*Congratulations*" and The Manhattans', "*Kiss and Say Goodbye*," I must have finally fell into a deep sleep, and now his no good ass has the audacity to even mess that up.

The rest of the holiday weekend went by uneventful as usual, he kicked it with his homeboys, my girl Shayla was busy getting dicked down and I was wallowing in my misery, giving my undivided attention to my forth pint of Pecan Praline.

Tuesday morning couldn't have come fast enough, instead of leaving the house at my usual time of 8am; I was up and out the door by 6:45am, ready to escape the tragedy that had become my life. By the time my assistant, Maya, got to the office at 9am, I had three proposals on her desk waiting for her to have them hand-delivered over to some high-profiled clients I had been courting for a while. As I sat down and kicked my

Jimmy Choos underneath my desk and began rubbing my toes, a trait I've done since childhood, when I'm in deep thought; I thought about how fast I've climbed the career ladder and how if I can seal at least two of these big wig accounts, I'll be in prime position to snag the promotion I so desperately wanted. Maya taped lightly then entered my corner office, overlooking the brilliant Atlanta skyline. "Ms. Pearson, Mr. Samuels has called an emergency board meeting and would like everyone in the conference room in 15 minutes. Is there anything you need me to gather for the meeting?"

"Thanks, Maya, if you could just grab me a double caramel latte, that would be great. I have been grinding so hard that I haven't had the chance to get my caffeine fix on this morning and lord only knows what Samuels might be throwing our way, so a sistah has to be ready." As I sat back and closed my eyes briefly, I wondered why is it that the vain of my existence is this fucking job? It seems to be the only thing in my life at the moment to bring me any kind of excitement. Lord, what has my world come to?

"Honestly, Maya," I said after returning from the impromptu meeting, I think Samuels just likes to hear himself talk. He calls those meetings just to assert his fucking authority.

Closing the door, Maya said, "Girl, who you telling!" As we exchanged high fives, she went on to say, "Looks like he would sit his little, stubby ass down somewhere. Everybody and their mama knows the only way he got that position was because that half-fat wife of his is the CEO's grand-daughter, and money or not, he was the only one stupid enough to marry her ugly ass!"

I was literally laughing so hard; I almost peed in my pants. "Girl, you are a fool, " I managed to say between bouts of hysteria. "And her ugly ass has the audacity to be biggity! Sometimes, I just wanna say, "rich or not, Bitch, you too damn ugly to look down your nose at any damn body!"

"Noooooooooooo," Maya screamed! "But that's not even the worst part; the worst part is her ugly ass got the nerve to think somebody want Samuels' stank ass besides herself. Yuck! She comes up in here and be looking me all up and down, anytime he's around. I want to say, "Ho, it ain't enough money at the US mint for his fat ass to even get a look at this! I wouldn't fuck his short, stubby ass with somebody else's pussy!" At this point, I was laughing so hard, tears were running down my face, my nose was snotty and my stomach was cramping like crazy from trying to hold the sound inside before the entire office heard us.

Maya McDaniel, now Maya Jones, my girl Maya, aka...M&M, has been the same every since I've known her. We met our freshman year over at Spelman. Her dorm room was across from mine, Shayla's and some trick named, Tameka Ferguson. Half way through our freshman year, after Tameka's trifling ass had tried Jonathan, Shayla's flavor of the month and Kevin, the love of my life, we'd kicked her skank behind out and moved Maya in. That is, after Maya had whipped her ass...hood style!

Let me start from the beginning. Maya and I were not what you would call friends because we barely knew each other. Although, we had seen each other around campus and in the dorm and were polite to one another, we'd never really had the chance to kick-it though because all my spare time was spent with Kevin.

KEVIN 3

KEVIN Williams was my high-school sweet heart and the love of my life. We both moved to Atlanta to go to college after we graduated from Northside High School in Macon. Our plans were to graduate from college, me as a Chemical Engineer and he with a degree in Education, which he never intended to use because he was supposed to go to the NFL as a first round draft pick in his senior year. We were always friends but when we were sophomores in high school, our friendship blossomed into something special. In the beginning, the first year or so, we were inseparable, wherever you saw Kevin, you saw Nicole and vice versa. If I was at church, HE was in the choir stand. If HE was on the football field, I was on the sideline in a cheerleading skirt. If I was shit, HE was flies on shit...you get the picture. Kevin wasn't drop dead gorgeous or anything, but don't get me wrong, he damn show wasn't ugly either. He had this air of sexuality that floated around him like an aurora. His personality was like a magnet that just seemed to attract everyone to him...and that became our biggest problem. Once united, he and I became quite a popular item in our neck of the woods, cause your girl was the shit too...if I must say so myself. That magnetism I so adored about Kevin then became my biggest problem, because he attracted whores from everywhere. Young, old, schoolteachers, and church ushers, my next-door neighbors, literally, Every-Damn-Body, for real! Now that I think back, I got that bastard more pussy than he ever got himself!

I guess that old saying is true, because nobody wanted his ass until I got him! That's one reason why I won't ever consider dating an ugly man. I used to always listen to the clients in my mom's beauty shop; well it wasn't really a beauty shop, especially by state board standards; just the back room of our section 8 apartment that my mama used to do hair. They used to say, "you can take the nastiest, ugliest drunk in the street, clean him up and give him a little pussy and before you know it, every bitch in the streets will be trying to throw him some pussy too." Now, they said a lot of ignorant shit in that beauty shop, I mean, back room...but that right there was no lie and I'll be damned if a ugly brotha is going to dog Nikki! Oh, no mam!

Well, to make a long story, short... even with all the drama in our young lives, Kevin and I, were just like my ass cheeks, we stayed together. After graduating, we both headed to HOTLANTA, he had a football scholarship to Georgia Tech and I had a full-ride, academic scholarship to Spelman. By this point in our relationship, I had sadly grown used to the other women. My self-esteem had taken a major blow because like many women who have been cheated on, I thought there was something wrong with me. Young and dumb, I still thought Kevin was the best thing since sliced bread and although he screwed around, I was the only woman he would claim as his own. So, I stayed.

Despite Shayla's, my best friend since 3rd grade,

insistence that I deserved better and Kevin was a piece of shit, I stayed. Despite, all the men, straight anyway, on Morehouse's campus trying to get my number every time I left my room without Kevin, I still stayed. Yes, did I forget to mention that Spelman was a Historically Black, all girls' college. Again, Kevin's bright idea, he didn't want me around other men. Stupid me, and my girl, Shayla, just took one for the team! She just spent most of her time on the campuses of Morehouse and Morris Brown, because as she would always say, "I'm strictly dickly!" Despite, some white chick claiming she was pregnant with Kevin's baby by the end of our first semester, my gullible ass still stayed.

However, on a breezy February afternoon, February 15, to be exact, of our sophomore year, I was walking back to my dorm from the library, when I heard sirens and saw more police lights than I had ever seen in my life. And growing up on the south side of Macon, I'd seen my fair share of blue lights. The first thought that came to my mind was whoever in the hell pulled that fire alarm in order to sneak some dude out their room got one more cussing out coming their way because I am tired as hell. I'd been up all night celebrating Valentine's Day with Kevin and I know he 's probably in my room still playing Silk's, "Freak Me, Baby," waiting to hit it one more time before he sneaks back over to his dorm. And on top of that, I still had to finish writing a five thousand-word essay for Lit 2 before my 8:00 class. Shit! And the fire department ain't even here yet, and I know they're going to take their own sweet time sweeping the building because they already know ain't no damn fire, somebody had just got a quick nut and couldn't sneak past the RA without getting busted. We go through this shit at least twice a week. But as I got closer to the building, I could see a lot more commotion than usual, then I heard Shayla's voice screaming, "Let her go, let her go! Pig, get your hands off of her!" All I could think was, "what the hell"!

I ran over to where the officers were trying to put Shayla in the back of a squad car, yelling "Officer, Officer, what did she do, why are you arresting her? "

The officer spun around to sneer at me; his face was beet red, he asked gruffly, "Miss, do you know her?" I slowly shook my head, even though I wasn't sure if I knew her ass or not, because the rambunctious vigilante that I was looking at, had replaced my best friend. As long as I'd known her, I'd never seen Shayla act that way before. She was always quick to say, "I'm a lover, not a fighter." The officer said, "Well, you better try to talk some sense in her head before we have to haul her ass down to the precinct for disorderly conduct and she can kiss this little education thing goodbye!"

I quickly shook Shayla, who was now starring blankly into the car in front of us, with tears rolling down her face. "Shayla, what's wrong with you, what happened?" She began to cry uncontrollably and I could not make out anything she was saying. So, I followed her gaze to the squad car in front of us as it began to pull off.

Finally, I was able to put her words together, she'd said. "He-lp MM-A-YA!" Unable to fully comprehend what had happened, I just watched Maya's angry eyes grow dimmer and dimmer as the squad car drove out of sight. Then more sobs in the distance, drew my attention away from Maya's departing gaze. My roommate Tameka was sitting on the curb with my bedspread wrapped around her naked body talking to a female officer. Confusion captured my mind but then I felt that magnetic force that I knew so well drawing me. Kevin. Blood running down the right side of his face, stared straight at me, almost naked, with the exception of my Spelman bath towel wrapped around his mid-section, standing next to another officer, who was writing something in his note pad. The officer followed Kevin's eyes over to me as he mouthed the words, "I'm sorry, Bae."

BFF'S 4

WORD spread around campus like wildfire, and it didn't help that Fox 5 news did a breaking news story on the "Sordid Love Life of GA Tech's Football Phenom." Thanks to Shayla's dad, Martin Daniels, III, the local news stations and the Atlanta Journal Constitution were issued a gag order and were unable to use mine or Maya's name during their reporting of the incident. I was merely referred to as Kevin's "significant other" but nothing could make the pain I felt any less than significant. Although, Maya had to spend the rest of that night in custody, thanks to Mr. D, as I've affectionately called Shayla's dad for as long as I could remember, she was released on her own recognizant. After hours of questioning, with Mr. D. by her side, Maya was released from Atlanta City jail around 6am the next morning. We, Shayla and I, along with Mrs. McDaniel, Maya's grandmother, waited relentlessly until she was released from custody. Watching Maya's grandmother pace back and forth, praying for hours made me feel like the dumbest woman that ever walked the face of the earth. If it were not for my stupidity, the sixty-two year old woman would have been home, in her Decatur housing complex, sleeping peacefully with Maya's two younger brothers in the next room. Instead, here she was, with her grandsons, Mylick, 15 and Myron, 13, fast asleep on the precinct benches, pacing back and forth, praying her eldest grandchild, first generation college student had not messed up her future by coming to the defense of my gullible, love-sick, country ass! I kept apologizing, all I could say was, "I'm so sorry, I'm so sorry." And she'd just hug me simply saying; it wasn't my fault, that's just who Maya was, that's who she's always been and that the Lord will have mercy on her soul.

By the time Maya and Mr. D. walked from behind those locked precinct doors, I thought I had aged twenty years. Shayla and I waited behind Mrs. McDaniel, now known only as Me-Ma to both Shayla's and my family, until it was our turn to embrace Maya. We hugged and cried so much that an officer came around and asked Mr. D if he could escort us out of the precinct because we were causing a commotion. That was the last time either of us have been inside of a police precinct.

As we veered away from the adults as they discussed Maya's fate, I asked Maya, "Why did you do what you did, you don't even really know me?"

At first, she dropped her head and remained silent for a second, and then she looked at me point blank in the eyes and said, "Because you didn't deserve that and I don't like to see good people being taken advantage of." According to Maya, and half the residents in Sampson Hall, every time Shayla and I were both out of our room, Kevin would miraculously show up and stay for hours. Maya said, she'd cornered Tameka off in the showers a few weeks earlier and told her point blank that she was going to kick her ass if she didn't stop messing around with Kevin behind my back and grinning in my face. But she said, Tameka had her little entourage with her and spouted off something like, "Your little ass need to mind your own damn business." And while Maya was barely 5'1 and 100 pounds soaking wet; her word was her bond and she meant exactly what she said.

Maya said, "As soon as you left to go to the library yesterday, Tameka miraculously appeared from her friend's room on the 2nd floor. Once she went into the room and never came back out, I figured Kevin must have been in there. I told myself I'd had enough, so I walked across the hallway and burst into your room.

They didn't even hear me come in, that whore was riding Kevin's dick, in your bed and I just lost it," she said. "I snatched her trifling ass off him mid stride and slung her up against the wall, then the ho fucked up and lost her balance and fell, that's when I jumped on top of her and went to work like Layla Ali or some shit. By this time, everyone was running into the room to see the fight. Eventually the RA and her boyfriend were able to get inside but when they couldn't get me off of Tameka, they called the cops. But before the cops made it all the way up the stairs, I jumped off Tameka's trifling ass, grabbed the prom picture of you and that asshole and ran over to the bed where he was still sitting all smug and amused, and broke the picture frame against the right side of his face. I cut his bitch ass to the white meat," she said laughing. "Then while the cops were dragging me off his bitch ass, the next thing I knew, Shayla ran into the room and started taking it to his bitch ass too. I was like, "Damnnnnnn!"

I looked over at Shayla, who had been silent while Maya was recounting the current events. "Okay, Shayla, what gives, you should be used to his shit...why were you so pissed?"

Looking back at her dad and Me-Ma, Shayla looked up with unshed tears in her eyes, reached in her pocket and pulled out a pregnancy test...the positive one I'd thrown in the garbage can earlier that morning.

BREATHE AGAIN 5

AS I was leaving work that afternoon, I decided to take a brief detour. I headed over to Lennox to pick up something sexy to try to get things turned up in my household. Although, Steven and I are rocky right now, I know he's a good man. When he's not putting his tired ass friends or his clingy ass mama first, he's the perfect man. Now, I'm not one of those dumb broads that like to brag about what their man will or will not do, because my mama taught me a long time ago that you can't put shit past no ho. She always said as long as they got a dick between their legs, they got a pre-disposition to fuck up because they've got two heads...and most of the time, they think with the wrong damn one! Just as I was about to check out the new bra and panty sets in Victoria Secrets, my cell rang. Usually I don't answer calls from blocked numbers but for some strange reason, I felt compelled to answer. "Hello," I answered tentatively.

A quite spoken voice stammered over the line, "Hel-hello, ma-may I speak to Nicolette Pearson?"

"Yes, this is Nikki Pearson, how may I help you?" Whoever this was had definitely piqued my interest because no one had called me Nicolette in years, hell; I think my own mama has even forgotten that she gave me that God-awful name. I have always hated it and from the time I could speak, I dared anyone to call me that...except

Kevin. Hell, even the student loan people called me Nikki.

The quite spoken voice drew me back to reality when he cleared his throat, "Mrs. Pearson, um um." Damn, dude, what is it, I'm thinking. Like he was reading my mind, his next few words were rushed out, as if he would chicken out if he did not hurry and get it on out. "Um, Mrs. Pearson, my name is Jermaine Davis and I'm calling about your daughter."

For a moment, I was taken aback. "My daughter...sir, I don't have a daughter. I think you have the wrong number." Everything in me wanted to hang up the phone, but then again, everything in me wanted to hear what the man had to say. Just in case...

"Mrs. Pearson."

"Please, call me Nikki, even my mom wasn't a Mrs." In my mind I mumbled to myself, "only because my sorry ass daddy didn't care enough to give her his name," but of course I didn't let that shit slip out. This poor man would have thought I was a damn fool.

As if on queue, he stammered on, "Mrs. Pear--- I mean Nikki, I don't mean to invade your privacy but I do think I am speaking to the right person. I know this is quite personal but by chance, are you the same Nicolette Pearson that gave birth to a 7llb, 9 0z baby girl at Grady Memorial Hospital in Atlanta, GA on November 15...?"

Before he could finish his question, I had already lost my balance and was spiraling head first against the iron rack;

housing some of the sexiest black thongs I'd ever seen.

"Mam, are you okay?" The store clerk said reaching out to catch me from falling and making a complete ass of my self, in the now packed lingerie shop.

Now, I was the one sounding like Bugs Bunny, stuttering and shit, "Th-th-thank you, dear. I'm okay." I turned around and damn near ran out of the store. I know the on-lookers were wondering what the hell is wrong but all I could think was that I needed to get some air. Sitting on a nearby bench, I dropped my head down between my legs and took fast, sharp breaths like my life was dependent on my next one. When I finally regained my equilibrium, I realized I still had the cell phone to my ear. I heard the man on the other line and for the life of me, I couldn't remember what the hell he'd said his name was. The quite-spoken voice was now a strong, masculine voice, yelling my name, "Nikki, Nikki, are you okay? Say something, Nikki, please say something!"

Sounding like a mouse, I meekly muttered, " Yes, I'm still here."

"Mrs. Pears-, I mean Nikki, I'm so sorry for contacting you like this out of the blue and if I had any other option I wouldn't, but I need, no, we need your help. Chelsea and I need your help."

At that very moment, my heart stopped. "What's wrong," I yelled. "What's wrong with my baby?" "Is she okay?"

The next few seconds felt like an eternity, my mind drifted back to the day I finally went into labor. About 6am that morning, I felt one hard pain, like the baby had just said, fuck it, I'm getting out of here one way or the other. The pain was so severe that I yelled out in agony, and just as they'd been all summer, Shayla and Maya were by my side before I could get my next word out. Shayla screamed when she saw the puddle of water on my sheets, "Your water broke, we're having a baby, we're having a baby!" Her eyes were so filled with excitement and joy, as if she were the one about to deliver a precious baby of her own. Maya and I exchanged glances, I shook my head, "no" to try to stop Maya from breaking her promise but the last shriek Shayla made caused Maya to burst into tears, which if you knew her, you'd know this was very uncharacteristic of her. Shayla, being the sheltered youth that she was, still did not realize something was wrong; she sauntered over to Maya, who was sitting in the armchair at the foot of the cramped, full-sized bed we all shared, and hugged her, "It's okay to cry Maya, it's happy tears, we're having our beautiful baby today and everything will go back to normal."

As she got her last words out, Maya began to shake her head, "Nooooo, noooo."

I finally spoke up, "It's okay, Maya, I'll tell her."

Shayla turned to me with a look of confusion on her face, "Tell me what, Nikki? What's going on here?"

This was only the first time I'd actually said the words

out loud, so they got caught in my throat, I whispered, "Shayla, we're not going to be able to bring the baby back here."

"Oh, that's okay. Macon ain't but a skip and a hop; we can gas Susie up and go see the baby everyday. And I know when we have to study for finals, your mom can bring the baby up here to see us and..."

Cutting her off, I said a little more sternly, "No, there's not going to be a baby at all, I'm giving it up for adoption."

Shayla looked from me to Maya, then back to me before she finally spat," What!" "What are you talking about?" "You can't do that! You can't just give our baby away!" And with that, the baby kicked ferociously inside me and I doubled over in pain. By the time we made it down to Grady Memorial, me in the ambulance and Shayla and Maya trailing closely in Susie, I had dilated six centimeters, everything from that point went so fast. Even though I was in the most severe pain I'd ever felt in my life, the only thing I could think about was the pain in my heart. First, I'd lost Kevin and now I was losing my baby too. Once, I felt the head come through my vaginal canal; I waited, holding my breath, for what seemed like a lifetime for the baby to cry. Just as I was about to panic, I heard it for the first and the last time...the sound of my baby's voice. Then I lost consciousness.

Hearing the voice in my ear brought me back from a dark place, "She's okay...but she needs you." I didn't realize it, until I almost choked, gagging for air. I had been holding my breath; just as I had in that cold, damp delivery room six years earlier.

SHAYLA 6

AS I pulled into the driveway of my 3400 square foot, four bedrooms, four-bath home, my mind was spinning in a thousand different directions. Madame Cleo could not have told me when I left home all gong-ho this morning that this is how my day would end. Instead of celebrating the closing of at least two, new accounts for Globalnomics Industries, I was sitting in my driveway, biting my nails, just like I had in 3rd grade when I sat in the principal's office waiting for my mama to come pick me up because I had got caught cheating on a math test.

That same feeling of dread, anxiety and uncertainty that I felt as I waited on Barbara Pearson, aka, Mama Dearest, to come pick me up to serve out my three day suspension was like waiting on Satan to give you some ice water at the gates of hell. I knew my life was over cause mama didn't play that! As I sat there, biting my nails, in walks another young girl about my age. She sat across from me in the little blue chairs, crossed her legs and started humming Michael Jackson's, '*Thriller*," I looked up from my nail biting in shock. Thriller? Really? Did she miss the fact that she was in the principal's office, where the fuck is the thrill in that? When she noticed me starring dumbfounded in her direction, she said," Hi, what's your name?" Small talk? Really? In the principal's office? You gotta be fucking kidding me! When I just looked at her like she was crazy, without opening my mouth, you would have thought she would have gotten the point, but nooooo, she gets up and come sit in the chair next to me and say, "My name is Shayla. Don't worry about anything, I'm in here all the time, it's a piece of cake." I looked at the girl like she had three heads and her named was fucking Medusa! She snatched the pink slip out of my hand and said, "What did you do and who's on their way to pick you up?"

I finally looked up, now with tears streaming down my face, "Cheating. My mama."

She put her arm around my shoulder and said, "Don't worry, I got your back." And just as she was getting the words out good, a man sauntered into the principal's office looking like Denzel himself. He stopped and chatted with the receptionist, Ms. Jenkins, but we called her Ms. Fassass. She always wears short, tight skirts and is always prancing around the men in the school, janitors and all. One day she came into my class to see, Mr. Harris, my history teacher. But instead of standing by his desk and talking to him eye to eye like everybody else, she bends her hot ass over the desk and talk to him. I remember thinking, my mama and the ladies in the shop would tell you to get your fass ass from over that desk like that. So, from then on, I called her Ms. Fassass and all the other kids did too.

Just as Ms. Fassass was about to turn up her flirt meter on Denzel, he looked over in our direction and said, "Shayla, what have you done now? What do you have to say for yourself?" And as if on queue, Shayla, who had just been sitting in the principal's office, jamming to Thriller loud enough for the whole damn office to join in, turned on the water works like she'd just buried her great-grandmother. I could not believe my fucking eyes; I said to myself "look at this shit!" If I had tried that bullshit with Mama Dearest, she would have knocked my damn teeth down my throat. And the Oscar goes to... she had this dude eating out of her hands. By the time, she was finished with Denzel, I mean, her dad, Shayla had him wrapped around her finger. Then she told him that she was the reason that I was in trouble and now my mama was going to kill me, all because of her. I was stunned. Then she burst into tears again...damn, she was good. I was literally watching this shit like I was on the set of mama's favorite soap opera, The Young and the Restless. All I needed was somebody to yell, "CUT"!

A few seconds later, when Barbara Pearson burst into that office, I knew all hell was about to break loose and even a Broadway play couldn't stop her from killing me on the spot. Before the principal could step in front of her, she had grabbed me by my flannel shirt, "Cheating, oh so you want to cheat? You just like your cheating ass daddy." And on queue, Shayla burst out crying so uncontrollably, you would have thought she had to go home with Mama Dearest.

Of course, mama was not the least bit fazed, she just turned and looked at her ass and was about to turn her attention back to my little ass squirming in the air, when Denzel, I mean, Shayla's dad, said, "Excuse me mam, my name is Martin Daniel, III;" and I kid you not, when my mama, who could probably whip the devil's ass on a bad day, looked up into the face of the handsome stranger that was interfering with her killing her only child in public, she actually giggled like a fucking school girl. I was in pure shock. What the hell did Shayla and her fine ass daddy do to my mama? In all my years, I'd never heard her giggle. Now, I had heard some strange sounds coming from her room at night when my sorry ass daddy graced her with his presence, but it sounded more like a wounded animal, it damn sure wasn't no damn giggles like this. Unfuckingbelievable!

I felt like I was having an outer body experience because I had never witnessed anything like this. I'm not sure if she had forgotten she had my little ass dangling mid air or if she just didn't give a damn, cause she dropped me like a hot straightening comb and reached her hand out all delicate and shit to shake the stranger's hand. Shayla's dad went on to explain that bull Shayla had fed him about how she was the reason I had gotten in trouble and how I did not actually do anything. It was his poor daughter, who was having a hard time adjusting to her new school and moving away from her family and friends. As for me, I just sat quietly on set like a got damn extra, cause this shit really was golden globe worthy and Shayla's conniving ass orchestrated the whole thing. Unfuckingbelievable!

As we exited the building with our parents, Shayla lovingly holding her dad's hand and me walking way behind my mama, just in case she snapped out of this trance soon and finished what she'd started in the principal's office. Before they walked on towards their car, Shayla dropped her dad's hand and came up to my mama and hugged her tight, then looked up at her and said with fresh tears in her eyes, "I'm so sorry Mrs. Pearson for getting Nikki in trouble, it'll never happen again!" My mama was absolutely speechless, and that was a fucking first! Her big mouth, know-it-all ass, always had something to say, even if she had to talk to her damn self. Then Shayla came and gave me a hug and said, "I'm sorry," Nikki. "Will you accept my apology?" All I could do was nod my head, "yes," because at this point, my extra role had no significance at all; Shayla's ass was better than Diana Ross playing Billie Holiday in *"Lady Sings the Blues!"*

We waved good-byes to the Daniels' and were on our way. Mama Dearest sang along with the radio all the way home. Just as we were turning into our housing project, none other than Michael Jackson's, *"Thriller,"* came on the radio, and mama really went to singing then, doing the little dance with her head and everything. Unfuckingbelievable.

STEVEN 7

"SNAP out of it, Nikki!" I said to myself as I realized I had been sitting in my drive-way for about ten minutes, holding the remote in my hand, day dreaming about my past. Once I pressed the remote and the mechanical hinge started rolling up, I couldn't believe my eyes. What in the world was Steven's ass doing home? Now, any other day, I'd be getting a call or a text about how he was going to kick it with this homie or that homie, or how his pill-popping mama needed him to do this or that, but today when I needed the refuge of the solitude of my home, that bastard had the nerve to be up in my shit. Unfuckingbelievable.

As I entered through the garage door, trying to fight off the feeling that had consumed me every since I'd answered the call from the private number, my senses were taken aback by something that rarely happened here, unless Maya came over. Someone was actually cooking in my house. What the hell? As I walked through the sunken family room, across the cold hardwood floors into the dining room, I could not believe what I was seeing. With the kind of day I'd been having, I thought it wise to close my eyes and open them again just to make sure I wasn't hallucinating. As I opened them again, No...I saw it right the first time. Steven was actually standing in front of the double oven in my chef's kitchen, removing two gorgeous rib eye steaks, smothered in mushrooms and wild rice, and two, huge, char-grilled lobster tails, my favorite meal. I was speechless, and just like my mama that shit doesn't happen often.

I was frozen! All those nights I had sat up in this big ass house by my damn self, waiting for this man; my man, to come home and show me a mere ounce of care and concern, and now here he is, when I should need him most, doing something I have only dreamt of and all I could do is stare at him like he was a fucking alien invading my got-damned planet. Suddenly that feeling I had been holding back, came up out of nowhere...and that feeling had a name...nausea. I ran to the downstairs restroom and called earl until there was nothing left to regurgitate. Steven sounded so worried, as he questioned me about what I had eaten today and if I was all right. After a few minutes of him standing there, he suddenly left the room. With my head still down on the toilet seat, I shook my head to myself, thinking, now that's the Steven I know...always hauling ass and always thinking about only himself. But then, I heard him walk back into the room, suddenly I felt a coolness on my neck. Is that a damp cloth on my neck? I wondered. And who the hell put it there? I know not Steven's selfish ass. The alien must still be here I thought, but then I felt him kneel down beside me, rub my back and whisper, "Babe, do you need me to call your doctor or do you want to go to the emergency room, you might have food poisoning?" Who the hell is this and what the hell did he do with Steven? The Steven I know sleeps in the guest room when I get a common cold, saying I might be contagious. Really, fool? My Steven, yes, the Steven I know, made me drive myself to the drug store to pick up my prescription after I'd had oral surgery and the doctor had just told him I had been heavily sedated and did not need to drive for a couple of days. Although the CVS was only about two miles away from the house, that was one of the longest trips I'd ever been on because I was so nervous I would hit someone because I was so damn drowsy. I could have called one of my girls to go run the errand for me, but I was too embarrassed to let them know that I couldn't even depend on my dude to do the bare minimum for me. When I finally made it back, an hour later, that bastard had the nerve to ask me if I had remembered to pick up him some more deodorant because he was almost out. I just stared at his selfish ass and once all hell had ran through me and the Mama Dearest came out, I hurled the sprite bottle I had been clutching at him, hitting him right on target, in that half-pint, limp dick of his. And while he rolled around on my couch, holding his nuts, screaming like a bitch, I sauntered up my stairs without a care in the world, just like Angela Basset, when she lit her husband's car and cloths on fire in Waiting to Exhale! My girl, Shayla, would have been so proud of my little performance.

Once I was sure there was nothing left to throw up, the alien helped me to my feet. He, the alien that is, picked me up and carried me up the stairs to my bed. First he just laid me on the top of my comforter, then I heard drawers opening and closing, but I was too dizzy to lift my head to actually see what was going on. Then he came back with a cup of Listerine and a plastic cup, held my head up, poured the liquid into my mouth and told me to gargle but not swallow. NOW, I know damn well this is an alien, cause Steven's favorite request is for me to swallow! Once he'd helped me cleaned my mouth out, I just knew that he was probably turned on by seeing my mouth wide open and vulnerable, I'm surprised he didn't try to stick his dick in it. Hell, sometimes he have me feeling like I'm merely a walking sperm bank for him, that dog would take some head every night of the week if I were that damn gullible. But not tonight, Steven, I mean, the alien, came back with a warm, damp cloth and wiped me off then pulled the covers back and placed my naked body on my fresh 900 thread count sheets and covered me back up. Once I was curled up in the fetal position, sleep taking over, I heard him, the alien, that is, humming the words to my favorite love song, "If I ain't Got You." And I might be wrong, but I could swear I heard him, say "I love you, Nikki," as I slipped out of consciousness.

BABY DADDY 8

MY baby needs me was all I could think about as I got dressed for work the next morning, Typically, I am a morning person, but for some odd reason, I could barely put one foot in front of the other this morning. As I stumbled into the bathroom, I could feel Steven's eyes on my ass. "Nah, Bruh, it ain't even happening," was all I was thinking in my head. I can't believe men; they would take a piece of ass in the middle of a natural disaster. I can see Steven's selfish ass now, "Hey God, my bad, but could you just let me hit this right quick, then you can finish judgment day." Selfish bastard! As I began brushing my teeth, the nausea returned with a vengeance, I rushed over to the commode and let it ripped. Steven ran inside the bathroom and stood beside me like a scarred little boy about to piss his pants. "Babe, I really think you should go see a doctor today." All I could do is moan in compliance. Then he said, "Do you think you could get Maya or Shayla to drive you, I am supposed to meet my boy, Tyrik, in Buckhead around noon and you know how long those doctor appointments can take." I just looked at him, yep, that's the Steven I know. Instead of going to the doctor, I took two Benadryl and lay back down and that's where I remained for the next two days.

What the hell is all this ringing in my head, am I dying? I sat up in bed and looked around my room, I was so dizzy; I literally had no idea where the hell I was or how in the hell I had gotten there. Then the incessant ringing began again. The doorbell, oh, snap, that's what that is. But who on earth could be at my door, no one even knows I am home. As I stumbled down the stairs towards the front door, I glanced at the kitchen counter and saw it was a complete mess. I know good and damn well, that bastard don't think I'm cleaning up that shit. Oh, hell nawl! Once I made it to the front door, instead of asking "who is it", I peered out the pep hole because today was not the day to be dealing with those aggravating ass Jehovah witness that patrol the neighborhood, passing out literature. I have to give it to them, though; they are ride or die for the cause. I have never known of any other religious group to be so persistent in recruiting more believers. I should have known, as I opened the door, Maya's little ass was still jamming my doorbell, actually holding it down with her elbow. Where they do that at? Nobody but Maya, anybody else would have left, but this heifer had no clue on how to take "no" for any answer. Still sitting in her powder blue Mercedes CLK, Shayla was applying some MAC lip-gloss to her already luscious lips, totally oblivious to everything around her. I know this impromptu drive-by was one of Maya's bright ideas. My girl, Maya! "Maya, what are you heifers doing here and why are you not in the office, watching my damn back, you know how those vultures down there would love to de-throne a sistah.

"Man, forget them, ain't nobody got time for that!" As she barged her way in, pushing me aside in my own house, she beckoned towards the driveway for her sidekick to follow her lead. So I stood anxiously by the door waiting for Shayla, the diva, to sashay her designer ass into the house. Keep in mind; this shit took all of five whole minutes because no matter the audience, this heifer always put on a stellar performance. "Bitch, bring your ass on here, ain't nobody here to see your ass but us," Maya yelled. Unfazed, Shayla merely waved her hand in Maya's direction and kept sauntering into the den. Maya began, "First, of all...what the hell is wrong with you? Why have you not been to work and better yet, why haven't you been answering your phone?" Before I could muster up and answer, she began again, "And why the hell did we have to hear from Steven's trifling ass that you just been sitting over here in the dark, crying and throwing up and shit. The last time you did that, you were..."

"Oh, my God, Nikki! No!" And now the show begins... lights, camera, and action. As if on queue, Shayla fell back on my leather couch all dramatic and shit with her hand over her forehead.

"Say something, Nikki," Maya warned. "Before Marilyn Monroe over there goes in for act 2." Looking across the room at Shayla, she rolled her eyes so hard I could feel it in the pit of my stomach. But of course that shit didn't faze Marilyn, cause that nut was still lying over there lifeless with her damn eyes closed and her hand over her head for effect. Stellar.

The whole scene was so crazy; I could not help but to burst out laughing. I needed these two fools so bad and they did not even realize that although they are crazy as hell, they are the only reasons I stay sane. Now, Marilyn has set up and is starring at me all wide-eyed and shit, probably because my laughter interrupted her award winning performance. And from the other side of the room, Militant Mini has crossed her arms in a defensive stance cause she's still pissed for making her worry. Looking at both of them, I knew everything was going to be all right. These two and Susie, my 96 Honda Accord, have always been the only things in life I have been able to depend on...I guess that's why I still hold on to that old ass car. Shayla, especially, has been dogging me out for years, "Why do you still have that old ass car?" She'd say, "Don't ever drive that piece of shit to my condo. If you don't drive your Beemer, don't bother about coming!"

Now that I think about, that is some stupid shit; I drive that raggedy old car, with no damn air conditioner, more than I drive my luxurious 2014 BMW 750li. As sleek as the automobile is, with its plush leather interior, easy handling, and hands-free controls, I still jump my happy ass in Susie and ride like I ain't got a care in the world.

I gingerly walked around to the couch and sat down, near where Maya was still standing. Since I had not eaten in three days, I was so weak; shoot, I could barely hold my head up. I took Maya by the hand as she sat on the arm of the chair; now if she was anybody else, I would have told her if she didn't get her ass off the arm of my $6000 white, ostrich leather couch I know something. My mama didn't play that shit, projects or not! Mama Dearest always said, "it don't matter if we live in a damn outhouse, that better be the cleanest outhouse you ever

been in and you better take care of what you got in it." I
used to be so damn tired of her having blankets or plastic
over all the damn sofas in the living room. I could never
understand it, because she went out and put a new living
room set on her bill at the local Farmer's Furniture every
five years like clockwork. Then complain that she got to
pay her furniture bill cause they wasn't about to come
pick her shit up for everyone in the projects to see. And as
soon as she finally gets the shit paid off, she brags about it
for the next three months, then she hops her happy ass
right back up in those white folks store going to get a new
set and put her stupid ass right back in debt again. Hell,
she could've kept the same set forever, cause she always
kept those ugly throw covers on top of it, so don't nobody
really know what the hell it looks like anyway. Besides,
we could barely sit on it unless we had company anyway!
That shit was crazy to me; yet, she could never figure out
why we could never get out the projects. Duh, cause you
ignorant, that's why! I love my mama, in my own way, but
that commercial was right when it said, "you could learn a
lot from a dummy." Cause my mama taught me some real
shit...that's why, when I want something, I find out the
cost and I save my money and pay for it cash. I have never
had any kind of furniture bill, when I use my credit cards;
I pay the entire bill off at the end of the month, as to not
pay any interest fees. My home and that damn BMW is the
only things that I have ever really financed, but my credit
rating was so high that I barely see an interest payment
and I always make sure to pay more than the monthly
installments on both to cut down the interest over the
lifetime of the loan, so I'll pay them both off a lot sooner.

Thanks, mom.

As I sat, holding Maya's hand, I motioned for Shayla to come over and join us, which I know that's what that nut was waiting on anyway because she wanted all the attention to be on her. She dramatically stood, casually sucked in a long, hard breath and treaded over to us like she was Michael Clark Duncan, walking the "Green Mile" and shit. If that fool get over here and say, "Okay, Boss," I promise I'm going to whip her ass my damn self!

Once the drama queen was seated, I also took her hand and as I sat there reflecting over all we'd been through and how these two had sacrificed so much for me, I knew I was blessed. Tears began to well up in the corner of my eyes, which in turn, made their eyes swell up, too. I started slowly, "First, of all...I am definitely not pregnant." I could see the stress run from both of their bodies,

Then Maya, the constant worrier, said, "Oh my God, are you sick. Please..." and before she could finish, she was crying uncontrollably.

Pulling her close, trying to console her, I said, "No, Maya, stop, that's not it. I'm not sick, okay, I'm not sick!" She finally stopped crying; bless her soul. I began again, slowly, "Three days ago, I got a call from a man named Jermaine Davis and..."

"And what?" Shayla spat, finally forgetting her performance. "Man, just tell us!" "Who the hell is Jermaine Davis?"

"My baby's daddy," I said quietly.

MY GIRL 9

I knew my "two live crew " was just what I needed. After I told them about the conversation I'd had with Mr. Davis, I felt so much better. As always, they provided the solace I needed. I guess from years of being raised by Mama Dearest, when things got to be too much for me to handle, I mentally shut down. Which is what I was on the verge of doing before they showed up the other day. I would literally lay down my life for those two because they have honestly saved my life. If I wasn't for them, I hate to think about what I would have done back then.

As promised, I called Mr. Davis back and agreed to meet him the following Saturday at Pappadeaux off Jimmy Carter. He said they were originally from New Orleans, so I figured this would be a great location for us to meet because they specialize in Creole Seafood. Not to mention, it just so happens to be mine and the "two live crew's" favorite spot to dine. Besides, the Swamp Thing might just be the antidote I need to help me get through meeting my daughter's adoptive parents for the first time. My emotions have literally been all over the place, no pun intended. Honestly, I have always known the day would come that the baby I gave away, would one day want answers to questions only I could provide. I just didn't expect the day to come so soon. For pete's sake, she's only six. But according to Maya, who is like the surgeon fucking general about everything child proof, since she gave birth to her twins, Shia and Khia, two years ago, kids are much smarter now than the generations before them. I guess they really are doing things faster; even six year olds are tracking down their birth parents this soon.

Damn, technology and social media done jacked up the world for everyone, that's why I don't do it! I have to agree with Mama Dearest on this one, social media is the devil. I don't have a Facebook, Twitter or Instagram, for real...ain't nobody got time for that! Shayla's ass stays on Facebook and Instagram more than she's ever stayed on any job she's ever had. Boy, if she could log those hours and get paid for them, she'd be one rich bitch...and not off of some man's money or Mr. D's. I just don't have time for that, by the time I put in ten hours a day at Globalnomics, dealing with corporate assholes, who still don't realize it's the 21st century and women really do have rights, the last thing I want to do is come home and get on a computer or a smart phone and keep up with everybody else's business. Shit, I have a tough enough time keeping up with my own business. But Shayla's my girl and I wouldn't change a hair on her head, she's perfect just the way she is. So if she likes it, I love it!

I'll never forget the day after Shayla and I returned back to school after our three-day suspension, I waited patiently for her outside of our elementary school. When I saw her dad's car pull up to the curb, I hopped off the stoop and ran to the curbside to meet her. I yelled out, "Good morning, Mr. D."

He grinned broadly as he pulled off, "Good morning, Nikki. You girls be good today."

As soon as he pulled off, we both started giggling and jumping up and down hugging one another. As we headed inside, I said," Shayla, can I ask you something?"

She said, "Sure, what's up?"

"Well, I was wondering, what did you really get sent to the office for the other day because I didn't see you with a pink slip."

Shayla just burst out laughing, then said "Oh, that...I was talking in class while the teacher was talking, so she told me to get out."

"But that means, you were not actually supposed to get suspended?"

Ever the performer, she just hunched her shoulders and said, "Shoot, I'd rather be sitting at home watching Nickelodeon any day than to be sitting in detention all day, so I just rolled with it." Then she took a bow.

"But what about your teacher, didn't she know you were not supposed to be suspended?"

Shayla just shook her head and placed an arm around my shoulder and said, "You've got a lot to learn, my dear!" "Did you or did you not see my little performance the other day?" I slowly shook my head, "yes", unsure where she was going with this. "Now, after what you saw...do you really think any teacher would care that I was gone for three days?"

She was right. But I told her, " I would care, Shayla."

And I would. My girl!

THIS has been one of the longest weeks of my life. I guess the not knowing what to expect is driving me crazy. I don't know if the Daniels' are going to like me or if they will think I'm an evil bitch for giving my baby up for adoption. Does my baby need a kidney or something...and that thought alone has made me revisit some unsolicited memories that I've fought hard to escape.... Kevin.

On top of all that, the alien invasion is definitely gone and Steven's selfish ass is back to his old self. He has not even noticed that I have been walking around the house like a walking zombie. My hair had been pulled back in a ponytail for the last two weeks and I haven't even attempted to put on any makeup, which I definitely need to add some color to this pale ass skin of mine, in its zombie state. I've asked myself so many times why I stay with his sorry ass and I can never come up with a plausible answer. I guess I just don't want to be alone; yet I'm constantly lonely as hell.

After talking with Shayla for about an hour, she managed to persuade me to go get this wig done and treat myself to a massage to release some of my tension. Although, I'd rather have some dick, the massage will have to do, because Steven's selfish ass ain't getting none of this.

While headed down Peachtree, towards the salon, I decided to do something I rarely do...call my mama. She answered on the third ring, as she always did. Her logic is, answering on the first two rings makes you seem desperate and she didn't want a damn soul on this earth thinking she needed them that bad, but ironically, she answered my sorry ass daddy's calls before the first ring was even completed. You talking about desperate, that's just plain, thirsty! But anyway. "What's up, Moms," I asked, sounding a lot more cheery than I felt.

"Well, I'll be damned...if ain't Ms. High and Mighty! Hey, ladies, it's my hotshot ass daughter on the phone, " I heard her yell to the hen house. I rolled my eyes so hard I gave myself a damn headache...see that's why I don't fuck with her.

"Ah, Ma, don't be like that, you know I'm just really busy all the time. Did you get that package I sent you the other day?"

"Hell, even Oprah still got time for her mama, oh, but I 'spose you think you better than Oprah, huh? Yeah, I got the package, but what the hell you think I can do with a hundred damn dollars?" Really. I knew I shouldn't have called because it's the same shit all the time and I really don't need this junk right now. Growing up, I envied Shayla and even Maya so much. Shayla was able to call her mom or Mr. D any time and they would drop whatever they were doing and give her the love and attention she needed. And although, Maya's mom was on drugs, and was constantly in and out of rehab, at least she made an effort and it was clear that she loved her children, even though she had a problem. And Me-ma, words cannot express the love that woman showed her grandkids. She raised all three of her grandchildren on her own without receiving any aid from the system or their dead-beat ass daddies. Mylick, the oldest, had enlisted in the Air Force as soon as he graduated high school. He's now one of the youngest officers in the force; currently he's stationed in Arizona. He just had his first baby boy, Mylick, Jr. about three months ago. Maya took Me-Ma out there for the birth of M.J., while her husband Jason, with the assistance of myself and Shayla took care of Khia and Shia. Me-Ma said it would be a cold day in hell before she go back because it's too damn out hot there and she was never trying to get caught up in another one of those sand storms. She said she thought the world was coming to an end. I could just picture Me-Ma, looking like the mama from the movie Soul Food, getting caught up in a sand storm; I bet she was praying the entire time. Myron, who has become quite the ladies man, is a freshman at Auburn University on a full-ride football scholarship. Ugh, football. I hate football.

The screeching sound of mama's voice snapped me out of my reverie, and back to the selfish troll I call Mama Dearest on the other end of my line. She was going on and on about this person and that person, most of whom I don't even know or remember, but God-forbid if I tell her I don't remember them, that's when she'll say I think I'm better than folks. So, I hold the phone and say the appropriate, "Umm Hmm," "for real," "Sttttoooopppp" in the appropriate place and Barbara Mae Pearson was ecstatic. Pathetic, right, I wouldn't wish our mother/daughter relationship on my worst enemy...hell, even Jack the Ripper deserved better than this.

When I found a gap where she finally had to pause to take a breath, I said, "Hey mama, Maya is beeping in about work, I gotta go, I'll call you back."

"Oh, okay, baby...I'll talk...oh, I forgot to tell you, Kevin stopped by when he came to visit his mom last week." DAMN!

I should have known it was too good to be true. It never fails; I cannot have one conversation with her without her bringing up Kevin's name. Every since our break-up and my public humiliation, it's like she has taken great pride in throwing him in my face like I was the one that fucked up our relationship. Forget the fact that he had broken my heart for the world to see, I guess I was just supposed to grin and bear that shit. Two weeks after the incident, I went home to my mom's to find sanctuary from the reporters and gossips on campus, but what I got at home, from the woman that brought me into the world was worse than anything I could have ever endured in the streets.

Everyday I was subjected to having to wash hair in the hen house, just like I had to do from the time I was ten years old. Everything would be going fine, that is, until Young and the Restless went off at 1:30. Some kind of way, Mama Dearest would go from talking about Victor Newman and Katherine Chancellor, to my black ass. Really? What did one have to do with the other, but leave it to my mama, she'd always find some fucking way to relate it to my situation and then for the rest of the damn day, I would have to hear the advice from the hen house on how to keep a man satisfied. Really. Half of those bald-headed heifers in there didn't even have a damn man or at least not one to call their own. Ms. Johnson, who lived next door to us, was not fucking one, but two married men and had been for as long as I could remember. But she got the nerve to want to tell me something! Shit, thanks but no thanks, you can keep that shit to your self! And then there was Big Booty, Shirley; my mama's ace, "Nikki, baby, sometimes you just have to let a man be a man." Lord, what did she say that for...the hens really started cackling then.

My mama was the loudest one of all, "You shole' right bout' that, Shirley, cause having a piece of man is better than having no man at all, sometimes you just take what you got and work with it." She stopped pressing Mrs. Jones' hair and raised the straightening comb in the air for effect, smoke just circling, "You see, me and yo daddy, we been together for twenty years and I ain't worried bout him going nowhere. I don't care what he doing in them streets, he gonna always come home to mama. My mama used to tell me, if you go looking for trouble, you'd find it every time. That's why I sit my black ass right here, cause I know he's gonna always come back to the one he loves."

Oh she was on a roll now; she had an audience from her soapbox, all the other hens were at full attention. Some even had the nerve to stick their heads out from under their dryers so they could hear better. Hell, Big Booty Judy, who was the biggest hoe in the projects, had the fucking audacity to take the plastic bag off her permed head and Ms. Irene, who was as old as Medusa, reached up and took my hands out her head while I was trying to wash her damn hair! I hope suds get in her damn eyes. "Now, you listen and you listen good, cause your mama ain't gonna tell you nothing wrong. What you need to do when his fine ass call your stupid ass again, begging you to take him back, you better say, hell yeah. Cause, I can promise your ass this, them other bitches ain't gonna make his fine ass beg for a got-damn thing. You walking around here crying and shit, you better suck that shit up and go get your damn man, cause if you don't, another bitch will!" The hens went wild.

I packed my shit and left the very next day and took my secret with me.

SAME OLD LOVE 11

HANGING up the phone, I found comfort in listening to Anita Baker belt out "Same Old Love" from the surround sound system in my Beemer. Pushing Barbara Pearson's traitorous ass out my head, I sang along with Anita, like my next breath was dependent on it..."*From beginning to end, 365 days out the year, I want the same ole love baby. All I want to do, is share my life with you, I want the same ole love.*" Damn, is that too much to ask? Honestly, I'm inclined to really believe men are from Mars and women are from Venus, cause we are just entirely different. We think different, we act different, and we damn shole' love different. I just want someone that will appreciate me for who I am and who I am to them but it seems that's too much to ask. Men, always want their damn cake and want to eat it too.

For a while, I thought it was just us sistahs that were suffering from the lack of good black men, but after listening to Kristie, a Caucasian sistah of mine, hell, they ain't doing much better. I told Kristie that if things didn't work out between Steven and I, I might consider dating outside my race and she let me know point blank, race ain't got shit to do with it, assholes come in every color.

As I sat under the dryer after my two-hour massage, I tried to imagine how tomorrow's conversation with the Davis' would go. I suddenly grew more apprehensive than I've been in days. It's finally happening.

While pretending to be asleep the next morning, I watched Steven out of the corner of my eyes as he pranced his happy ass around the room getting dressed. I wonder where he's going? But I didn't ask, because questioning a man about where he's going is like suddenly dropping a nuclear missile on your biggest ally, just plain fucking stupid. Why couldn't I be fortunate enough to find a man considerate enough of me as his woman to just confide in me what's going on in his life? Before I make plans, I check with Steven. I always give him the heads up on my agenda. Is it so difficult to return the favor? It doesn't mean I'm trying to be your mama, just your woman.

I admit there are things that I think a woman should do for her man that I don't do for Steven anymore. But it wasn't always that way. When we first met, everything was beautiful. He did not rush me, he was patient and he listened to what I wanted and worked hard to make my wants a reality, and that's all I could ask. It wasn't his six-figure job that attracted me to him cause he didn't have one, it wasn't his charismatic smile that left me in awe; it was his attentiveness where I was concerned that won me over. Like most women, I, too, love the finer things in life but I need a man that knows that the little stuff may be more important in the long run. Sure, it would be nice if my man planned an impromptu vacation in the middle of the week, just to unwind. Or fly a sistah to New York during Fashion week and buy me some designer ensembles straight off the runway. But if you turn around and forget my birthday, it sort of diminishes that other shit. If our lines of communication only go in one direction, me talk and you pretend to listen...that's not good enough for me.

What happened to us? Oh, well. I rolled over, ain't nobody got time for that today. I closed my eyes, still faking sleep and waited until I heard the garage door close before I got out of bed. What a way to live.

DAMMNNN 12

I grabbed my cell off the bedside table, I don't know if I was hoping the Davis' would call to cancel or what. No missed calls, just two text messages, which I expected. My girls wishing me luck for today. They both wanted to go meet the Davis' with me but I told them this was something I had to do on my own. Although they didn't like it, they understood it.

As I began getting dressed, I wondered for the umpteenth time what the Davis' were like. I have never been so nervous in my life, and it's not like I'm even meeting Chelsea, I'm only talking to her adoptive parents. As I looked in the mirror at the Donna Karen stripped pantsuit I had chosen, I shook my head. "Too businesslike, I'm not going to work." With two walk-in closets full of designer cloths, I've never had a problem finding anything to wear, but today; it looks like a tornado had gone through my bedroom. With tears in my eyes, I finally played any-many-mighty-mo, and just picked one because I am smart enough to realize that I'm really chickening out and I know I owe my child more than that. I finally settled on a peach colored wrap dress that I brought last spring but never got around to wearing. After throwing a few curls in my hair with the ceramic iron and placing a tangerine gloss on my lips, I was satisfied. "Not too much, I'm not going to find a man." I was headed out my bedroom door when I suddenly remembered something I needed to do. I turned back, went around to my side of the bed, grabbed my bible off the nightstand and turned to the book of Psalms, 139:13-14. Although, I know the passages by heart, this has been my daily ritual since I fled the confines of my mother's home on that first day of March and decided to give my child life, and then provide it with a better life than I could ever give.

As I turned off exit 99, onto Jimmy Carter, my throat felt like I had swallowed a box of matches, it was so dry. The palms of my hands were so sweaty I had to be careful not to touch my dress. We'd agreed to meet outside of the restaurant in the waiting area right in front of the fountain, so we would not miss each other in the crowded restaurant.

As I got out of my car, I said a quick prayer and headed up to the courtyard. Once inside, I scanned the guest waiting around the fountain, there was a young white couple and their newborn baby, a couple of teens who appeared to be going to a prom, a fine chocolate brotha looking down at his shoes; I couldn't help but to think Shayla would be all over that. Then there was an Asian couple around on the backside, conversing with an elderly white couple, but I certainly don't think they were the Davis', he didn't sound white or Asian. Perhaps I beat them here, traffic could be a beast depending on the time or day or what direction you were coming from. I took a seat on the brick façade around the fountain, thinking to myself, "good, this will give me some time to get my thoughts together." Another ten minutes or so went by and no one approached the fountain that could be the Davis'. The original crowd that was there when I arrived had slowly dwindled down as their parties were called to enter the premises. The only ones left were the Chong family and Sexy Chocolate. I shook my head, thinking to myself, girl stop; you ought to be ashamed of yourself. First, you stereotyped this nice Asian family and you know how you feel when someone makes fun of your lineage and then you make a sexist comment about this man, who is probably a good, black brotha. Giggling to myself, but I bet their last name is really Chong or Lee, and as for Idris Elba over there, dammnnn! He really is sexy chocolate and if my girl were here, who ever the trick is that got his fine ass waiting would be out of gas! Looking in his direction again, I licked my lips thinking, fuck Shayla, if I were here under different circumstances, her ass would be out of gas!

I hope everything is okay with the Davis', maybe I should call Mr. Davis' cell, but then I looked down at my watch, it was only ten after. I had arrived early, which was a trait of mine. Again, Mama Dearest taught me that. I remember, I was about eight or nine and mama had an appointment with her food stamps caseworker. On her way down to the local Department of Family and Children Services, she got a call from my school saying they had found a gun on campus and were evacuating the school, so all the kids must be picked up as soon as possible. So my moms did like any mother would do, she hauled tail down to that school to get me, raising holly hell. By the time we made it back across town to the DFCS office, she was about five minutes late for her appointment. After making us wait for another hour and half, the caseworker finally came out in the waiting area to speak to my mom, not bothering to take us in her office. Even after mama apologized for her tardiness and explained to the caseworker what happened at the school and that she'd left her a voicemail, that caseworker still had the nerve to tell mama she had already closed her case for failure to show up for her review. Believe me when I say, all hell broke loose in that office that day; especially, when mama asked to speak with the supervisor and the little caseworker, one foot out of college and two feet out the trailer park her damn self, had the nerve to say, "You people always think the rules are going to bend for you." When I say, Mama Dearest turned it out up in there, that is an understatement! By the time we walked our black asses up out of there, not only did we have our food stamps, we had an extra $100 worth for our "inconvenience" and an apology from the caseworker, her immediate supervisor and the deputy director over Bibb County DFCS, whom assured mama that "something like this" would never happen in her county again. And, on top of that, my mama hasn't done another food stamp review since that day and her benefits arrive every month like clockwork. Barbara Pearson was a lot of things, but scared damn sure wasn't one of them.

Smiling at the memory, I looked around and it seemed I was the last one from the original group still waiting. I glanced at the new faces and the Davis' still appeared to be a no show. As I was getting up to move away from the band that was playing to call Mr. Davis' cell, I heard the hostess come over the intercom and call the Jermaine Davis party. So, instead of exiting the courtyard, I headed inside to the hostess stand. There were so many diners standing inside the tiny waiting area that I did not even bother to try to locate the Davis', I just made my way to the hostess stand. "Yes, I am with the Jermaine Davis party you just announced." She grabbed a menu and some silverware and led me through the crowded restaurant. Perhaps this wasn't a good idea. I thought. This place is so crowded we may not be able to hear each other. As the hostess bid me a good meal, she stepped aside so I could take my seat with the Davis' ...Sexy Chocolate...I mean, Idris Elba... I mean, damnnnnnn! Mr. Davis stood up to shake my hand. Suddenly, that little voice that had long ago taken up permanent residence inside my head was now sounding just likes Florda Evans from Good Times, "Dammnnn, Dammnnn, Dammnnn!" I'm going straight to hell...

MOTHER 13

"Mrs. Pearson, thank you so much for taking out the time to meet me to discuss Chelsea. I know this is difficult for you and I appreciate your willingness to hear me out."

Gathering my composure, I smiled and said, "Remember, you promised to call me Nikki and you don't owe me any gratitude, in fact I should be thanking you and your wife for doing for Chelsea what I wasn't able to do for her myself."

"Okay, Nikki. There is definitely no thanks required for that, I am blessed that God saw fit to give Chelsea to us. She has brought so much joy to our lives. I honestly felt like I wasn't living until she came into our lives six years ago."

I couldn't help but to think how blessed Chelsea was because I would give my life to hear my dad speak of me in this manner. There was no pretense, no chauvinistic air, just a man who deeply loves his child.

"I must admit, Mr. Davis---"

" That's Jermaine to you."

"I'm sorry, Jermaine. I must admit that I am curious about what you all need from me since you told me there is nothing medically wrong with Chelsea that would require you to track down her birth parents. So what is this all about?"

Clearing his throat, he picked up the menu, it seems in an effort to stall for time. "Would you like to order first before we get into the particulars of this meeting?" Looking over at him, I could see he was just as tense as I was, so I decided to go with the flow.

"Well, I suppose a drink would help to ease some of my anxiety," then I looked directly in his eyes and smiled...Lord, what the hell did I do that for, "and besides, your stalling tactics could use a little work." I laughed, he laughed.

"Man, am I that obvious, " he said between chuckles.

"I'm afraid so," I said laughingly and instinctively reached out and patted him on the hand. Lord, what the hell did I do that for, a bolt of electricity shook me to the core causing me to snatch my hand away like I'd been bitten by a snake. Stumbling over my words, I quickly said, "When the server comes back, would you please take the liberty of ordering me a Swamp Thing frozen daiquiri and an order of Oyster Pappadeaux for my appetizer, I'm going to run to the ladies room." As I began to stand, he came around and pulled my seat out... what a gentleman.

"Sure thing, mam. Will that be all for now?" With a smile and a nod of my head, I was gone.

As I entered into the packed restroom, my equilibrium was dwindling. I hurried to the handicap restroom at the far end, which I know is so wrong on so many levels, but I needed the space because I honestly thought I was going to hyperventilate. I have no idea where Mrs. Davis is but that broad better get here ASAP, cause I think I just flirted with her damn husband. "Oh, Lord," I said and threw my hand over my forehead in true Shayla form, "I really am going to hell!"

"Get it together, Pearson, this is about Chelsea, nothing more," I lectured myself as I headed back through the dining room. I was hoping his wife had joined the party, but as I approached our table, I could see it was still just he and I. And my Swamp Thing!

As Jermaine stood to pull out my chair for me he said, "She's a lot like you, you know. At that revelation, my heart stopped. I'd often wondered what my baby looked like, did it have my straight nose, or Kevin's lips...was it a boy or a girl.

Jermaine must have realized that what he said was affecting me terribly; he reached out and placed his hand on mine, and I know he had to feel that bolt too, but still he didn't remove it. Once I was able to will the tears back up, I looked up at him and a small voice escaped from my lips, "Really?"

Nodding his head slowly, his baritone voice began to speak softly as if he were singing a lullaby. "She is very perceptive, she pays attention to everything, and she is very sweet and considerate; almost to a fault. Even at six," he giggled a little, "you can tell she is extremely analytical; she questions everything and everyone as if to measure the quality of mankind. She is her own person and is not afraid of anything." At this point, I could not fight off the tears; I just let them fall and held on to his every word. "And she is so, so beautiful." Releasing my hand, he reached in his back pocket and pulled out his wallet. "Would you like to see her?" Not waiting for a response, he pulled out a picture and placed it upon the table. At this moment in time, I became oblivious to all the other patrons, the noise, the band... all I knew was that my lifeline had been lain on the table, two inches away from me and with shaking hands, I reached out to answer questions that had gone unanswered for almost seven years. I finally get to lay eyes on my child. When I looked down at the picture, soft sobs escaped my lips. There looking back at me were my eyes, my smile, my hair...my child.

After a few minutes had passed by, his voice broke in, "Keep it, I have plenty more." As the waitress approached our table with the appetizers, he made a light joke with her, so she would not notice my tears. Considerate.

As we ate in silence, we each lost in our own thoughts about this beautiful child, I felt relieved. She was well and she was loved. Thank you Jesus, I remembered Psalms 139:13-14.

"I must admit, these oysters are quite delicious, he said"

I looked over at him, "Oh, I just assumed when I saw that you'd ordered the same thing that you had eaten them before."

"Actually no, I am a big seafood lover but I typically

stick to steamed oysters, it's a man thing you know!"

Bursting out laughing, covering my mouth, making sure not to spit my drink all over him. "Oh, please don't tell me you believe that mess too?"

He was laughing so hard he had to take a big gulp of his sweet tea, " Well, growing up on the Bayou, I didn't want to take the chance of it being true and me missing out on it, so my Papa made sure all the Davis men acquired the taste for them at a very young age. I absolutely love them, I just have never had them prepared this way."

Raising my glass and tipping my head, "Well, I am so glad I was able to introduce you to something new." We laughed and took a drink.

"Are you ready to order," he asked, "And I'm not stalling this time," he chuckled.

"Well that's good to know, and for future references, you might want to leave great stalling tactics off your resume," we both laughed. "Seriously though, if you would like to wait a little longer on Mrs. Davis, I don't mind...this is all I have planned for today." With that, he dropped his head and his mood seemed to change. I hope I didn't say anything wrong.

Then he said, "What do you say we order our entrées to go, then go find a quite place so we can talk?"

Nothing about this man said I could not trust him,

"Sure, that will be fine." I actually saw him release a breath. Cute.

As we sat waiting for the server to bring out our to-go orders, he told me stories of Chelsea's antics in childhood. I was completely enthralled and overjoyed.

We googled nearby parks and found one about three miles from the restaurant and I followed him there. Normally, I would be very apprehensive about following a perfect stranger to a possible desolate area but everything inside me said I could follow this man to the end of the earth and it would be perfectly safe.

Once we got to the park, we found us a bench in pure sight but with a hint of privacy from the joggers, bikers and families playing on the lawn. As soon as we sat down he began, " I don't mean to keep prolonging the issue but I'm just so afraid of what you might say."

"Jermaine, listen, it is clear to me that you love Chelsea very much and I know I don't have the right to say this but I love her too, I have always loved her. Which is why I had to do what was best for her at the time. Now, when you called, you said my baby needs me and if that is true, then you just tell me what she needs and I will make it happen."

He looked me dead in the eyes and said as serious as I have ever heard anyone speak, "Chelsea needs you. She needs a mother, her mother!"

POOR BABY   14

"PERHAPS I misunderstood you, Jermaine," I said after a few minutes of trying to wrap my head around what he said.

"I don't want to beat around the bush, Nikki, and I want to be completely honest with you. So, let me give you a brief recap of how we got to this point."

"Okay," I said quietly.

"Eight years ago, my wife and I decided to start trying to begin our family. After being married for a year, we figured the honeymoon period was over and we had made it through that first trying year when most young marriages fail. Months into the natural process of trying to conceive and nothing happened, we sought professional help. After series of testing, the physicians could not come up with any medical reason why we could not conceive, so we kept trying, but nothing ever happened. So my wife, Deena and I decided maybe it wasn't meant to be so we decided we would adopt. After a few months into the process, we were contacted by an agency from Georgia stating that if everything went okay with the birth, then they may possibly have a baby for us that met our criteria. They delivered Chelsea to us when she was only three days old and for a while everything was perfect. However, the older Chelsea got, the more distant Deena grew.

"Oh, my God, why, what was wrong with Chelsea?"

"Nothing, dear, there was absolutely nothing wrong with Chelsea, there was something wrong with Deena. I had just been too blind to notice it before." Just as I was about to open my big mouth to ask another question, he held up his hand to stop me? "You can ask anything you want when I'm done, I don't want to miss anything." I nodded in agreement. He continued, "At first, the signs were small and I could not quite put my hand on what was going on. I just assumed Deena just lacked maternal instincts, mainly in part because Chelsea was not her biological child. When she requested we get a full-time nanny, I didn't think it was that unreasonable, we could afford it and Lord knows Deena was on the spoiled side; having been raised with a silver spoon in her mouth and all. So, I was cool with that. But I began to notice, once Trish, our nanny came on board, Deena stopped taking any interest in Chelsea at all and it was more than lack of parenting skills, it was if though she despised the child and the more attention I gave Chelsea, the worse Deena's behavior got. Chelsea was about three years old at the time and seemed to be oblivious to Deena's neglect; she just showered her love on those of us who doted on her; myself, Trish, my mother and my family. That revelation hit me like a ton of bricks one afternoon when Deena's mom dropped by. Normally when Chelsea would hear the doorbell, she would run and race Trish or myself to the door and when the door opened, she would give whoever it was a big hug. The mailman just loved it. Ours was the only house on the street that he actually got out and came to the door. Well, just so happened, when the doorbell rang that particular day, it was my chance to go through our race ritual with Chelsea. So, she jumped off my lap full speed ahead and I chased behind her, and once I slung the door open, Virginia, Deena's mother was standing there smiling. But instead of Chelsea bestowing her with her wonderful hugs and kisses, the child turned around and waddled back over to where we had been sitting and awaited my return. This did not seem to strike anyone else as odd but it struck a chord with me. Virginia greeted me with her usual peck on the cheek, spoke to Trish who had just entered from the kitchen and proceeded over to her daughter and began carrying on conversation as usual. Not once did she even acknowledge my child's presence. So, me, being the real nig...oh, my bad. Me being the man that I am, put her and her damn daughter out my house right then and there!"

"Are you serious?," I asked with wide eyes. All kind of hell was boiling in me but I was trying to stay cool.

"Hell, yeah, I'm serious! I called them out on it right then and there. I was so hurt but I was even more hurt for what my child had to be going through. Because for a three year old to be able to tell that her affection was not welcomed from someone, they must've really been cold to her, or worse. Sure, Deena and her mom tried to deny that they had ever mistreated Chelsea but abuse comes in many forms and oftentimes, emotional abuse is worse than physical abuse." His tears began to fall and so did mine. "That was the worst night of my life because I realized the woman I loved was not half the woman I thought she was. I cried most of the night, holding Chelsea tight on my chest as she slept. The next morning, I called my mom and told her what happened, but I still was so confused because I had no idea why. When my mom came by later that evening, she and I were sitting in the family room talking while Trish and Chelsea played in the next room. Once Trish had tired Chelsea out, she came and laid her on the couch near were I was sitting. She was sleeping like she didn't have a care in the world."

"Just as Trish was heading back towards the kitchen, she turned slowly and said, "Mr. Davis, I know it's not my place but may I say something?" She sounded so sad, my mom spoke up before I could, "Sure, Darling, you don't ever need permission to speak from anyone, you hear me?" With her head still dropped, she said, "Yes mam. Well, I know you have been trying to figure out why Mrs. Deena didn't love Chelsea and I think I know why." At this point I was ready to take any insight that I could get and logically Trish was a good source considering she was home with Deena and Chelsea more than I was because I worked sometimes 12 to 14 hours a day. I don't know why I hadn't considering asking her before now. Trish finally lifted her head and looked directly at my mother and me and said, " I think the reason she doesn't love Chelsea is because…she's not black enough." My mother and I shared the same reaction; we both jumped up and yelled, "What?" at the same time. I think we scared poor Trish, who was already shy and quite spoken; she jumped half a mile when we jumped up. I beckoned the poor child to come have a seat next to me, when she sat down, I grabbed her hand and lifted her chin, so that she could look me in my face and I said, "Trish, I'm not disputing what you're saying, I just don't understand what you're saying. So, if you don't mind, will you please explain it to us." With that Trish seemed a little more at ease and began to speak more assured. "You see, Mr. Davis, I have watched Mrs. Deena with Chelsea and she will play with her from time to time here in the house, so I don't think she hates her, she just don't know how to love her. She will never go out in public with her alone and when I'm with her, she makes sure I have Chelsea the whole time and when people walk up to us and plays with Chelsea and says how cute she is, Mrs. Deena, looks at me to say thank you. And I think it's because Chelsea looks more like me than she does Mrs. Deena."

My mother spoke up and said, "Why young lady, that is mighty perceptive of you to see such a thing, I would have never guessed that but it does have merit. How did you get that smart at such a young age? Trish just dropped her head for a moment with tears in her eyes, then she looked up and said, "I know because my grandma does me the same way." "So are you saying, you're not black enough for your own grandmother, " I asked Trish. "No, Mr. Davis, I'm saying, I'm too black for my grandmother, she's white."

As I listened to Jermaine talk so openly and freely, I appreciated the man in front of me. I asked, "Did you ever confront your wife about what Trish said?"

"The very next day," was his response. "I went and picked her up from her parents' home, we drove down to a nearby lake and sat on the car and we talked, more openly than we had in years. And Trish was right. Deena said she wanted to love Chelsea as her own but she just keep waiting for her to get darker and it never happened. She said her parents would call every other day or so and ask her if the baby's ears or knuckles were getting any darker or if her hair was getting darker or curling up and she said her answer was always, "no." She said she'd prayed about it, she even went back and looked at the spec sheet we filled out with the adoption agency about our preference and she just kept hoping the baby would get darker. I swear, sitting there listening to her, I could not figure out how I had never seen how superficial and flawed she was. Hell, I can love a human being, even if they were orange. This shit was just so crazy to me. How someone could not love an innocent baby because her skin was not dark enough just baffles the shit out of me until this day. And poor Trish, a grandmother not being able to love her own grandchild because of the color of her skin...Unfuckingbelievable"

"So, what happened with you and your wife?"

"She agreed on an amicable divorce settlement, if I did not publicize the real reason for our divorce. Can you believe that shit? A bigot and a racist of your own race but too embarrassed by it to want anyone to know." I could hear the anger in his voice. "I never spoke to her again after I dropped her back off at her parents' home that day and I never want to."

"Nikki, I know this is a lot and the last thing I want to do is interrupt your life. I don't know the reasons why you had to give Chelsea up at birth, but judging from what I have witnessed of you today and knowing Chelsea, I know you had to have some good reasoning for making the decision you made and again, judging from what I see, the decision didn't come lightly or without great sacrifice. My mother and my sister help me with Chelsea when I need it and I do the best I can by that little girl. I love her with all my heart and will lay down my life for her but as much as I wish I could, there are some things I just cannot give her, things she can only get from you. "

REALITY CHECK 15

INSTEAD of going home that night, I needed to be alone with my thoughts, so I took 85 to 75 and headed for the W hotel in Midtown. After checking in, I rode the elevator up to the 18th floor, found my room number, swiped my room key and escaped the reality of my existence. Before I headed for the shower, I picked up my cell, three missed calls from Maya, six from Shayla and none from Steven, and a text from Jermaine thanking me for listening. I texted Maya, I texted Shayla, I texted Jermaine but Steven...nothing.

I tossed and turned all night, thinking about how that evil witch and her mom mistreated my child. If I ever see her ass, I'm going to knock the black right off her ass, then let's see who is black enough then, Bitch! I held the picture of Chelsea close to my heart all night. I could not think about what Jermaine was offering me, without thinking about how it would affect all of those around me. What will my co-workers say? Shit, I don't give a damn; I don't like most of them any damn way. What would mama say? Ah shit, who gives a fuck, I certainly don't Then there's Steven. FUCK STEVEN. But then there's Kevin. What if he finds out we have a daughter. What will he do? Ah, FUCK HIM TOO!

Then I began taking inventory of those who do matter in my decision and how I think they would feel.

Taking inventory of all those that matter:

Shayla-CHECK!

Maya-CHECK!

Myself-CHECK, CHECK, CHECK,CHECK,CHECK,CHECK!

That settles it. I'm having a baby.

I picked up my cell, without thinking about the time and called my baby daddy. Jermaine answered before the first ring was done, "Hey You," he said.

"I hope I didn't wake you, but the answer is "Yes, Yes!" I started crying.

"Nikki, you have made me the happiest man alive. I can't wait for you to meet, Chelsea, you're going to love her." I already do, I thought.

"I am so excited about my decision, I wish I could jump in my car and go down to ToysRus and buy Chelsea all the things I'd dreamed about giving her," I told Jermaine. And he just laughed into the receiver. "For her birthday every year, my girls take me on a mini vacation, no matter what day of the week it falls on. When we were still in college, we had to be creative about where we would go, cause Shayla was the only one of us that had any money. So we'd do something like go downtown and stay in one of the hotels for a couple of days. Shayla usually had some idiot on stand by who was stupid enough to pay for a hotel room in hopes that he would get lucky. Then every year at Christmastime, I walked around ToysRus for hours, my first trip every season, I would shop for little girl items, befitting a child that would have been the same age as my baby, whom in my heart I was shopping for. Then the next trip of the season, I'd do the same exact thing, except then it would be for little boy items. I would take the gifts home, wrap them and put them under the tree until December 23, then I would take them to a local orphanage and drop them off with tears in my eyes. Only Shayla and Maya were aware of my ritual, but they never said anything, they just comforted me the rest of the holiday season."

"Wait a minute," he said, "So you never even knew the sex of your baby?"

"No, I only found out my child's sex when you called me and asked me about my daughter. I knew how much she weighed, how long she was, that she had all her fingers and toes, and her vitals were as they should be. I only knew I had a healthy baby, that's it. Shayla and Maya, held her, they took pictures, and they told her I love her for me, but they respected my wishes and never divulged anything. If they had, I would not have been able to let her go."

"Damn!" he whispered, "That's deep. I can't wait to meet this Maya and Shayla."

I giggled, "What was that all about?" he asked.

"Nothing, just that I bet they can't wait to meet you

either, " especially Shayla, I thought.

We talked until the sun came up, about everything. That was the best night I have had in years. I finally fell asleep around 7am, with my daughter's picture on my heart and a smile on my face.

It was about 3pm when I finally rolled out the bed, and if the maid had paid more attention, she would have seen the damn, "Do not disturb" sign on my fucking door! I guess it's hard to read though when you're on your cellphone talking ninety to nothing while looking over your shoulder to make sure you don't get caught. Oh well, I guess it's okay; I needed to get up anyway. Grabbing my cell, which was a morning ritual, I saw I had three missed calls, one from Maya, one from Shayla and one from...My Baby Daddy.

I called Maya and Shayla on three-way, so that way I wouldn't have to repeat myself or answer the same damn questions over and over again.

"Okay, Trick," said Maya. "You have had us waiting long-a-damn-nuff, now you better start talking or I'm going to come put my foot so far up your ass, the gynecologist won't be able to find it!"

"Calm down, Maya," snapped Shayla. "She just probably needed some time to let it all sink in." The drama queen being the voice of reason, damn, there is a God, I thought. "So, Nikki, start from the beginning, don't leave anything out, cause you know I have to visualize everything in my head, so I need every detail."

"First of all," I started. "Chelsea is so beautiful."

"Wait a minute, I thought they weren't bringing Chelsea?"

"No, Maya, she didn't actually come, but Mr. Davis, I mean, Jermaine gave me a picture of her and she is so beautiful! I just couldn't believe it, it was a dream come true."

"So how were the Davis'?"

"Damn, Maya, would you shut the fuck up and let her finish the damn story," Shayla yelled. "You fucking up my visualization. Go ahead, Nikki."

Well alrighty then, go Shayla. "Well, the Davis', where do I begin...hmmm, let's see... Mrs. Davis is a bitch that mistreated my baby and if I ever see her, I got something for that ass!"

"She did what?" They both shouted in unison.

"Okay, hold up, let me start from the beginning." I recounted the story that Jermaine shared with me the day before and finally got around to telling them why he wanted to see me. After I was done, the line remained quiet for a minute, and then Maya finally spoke up in what was barely a whisper.

"Oooh Nik, what are you going to do?"

"Well, that's the reason I checked myself in at the W last night and didn't call you guys, I just needed time to think."

"So, what did you come up with?", asked Maya.

"Well after I tried to figure how I could kill Deena Davis' black ass and get away with it. I wrote out a list of reasons why I should and reasons why I shouldn't. And how it would affect people other than myself."

"And..." said Maya.

"And I realized the only person that really matters is.... Chelsea. And the only reason I need is because she needs me!"

As if on queue, Shayla lets out this long screeching sound. "Ahhhhhhhhh." I guess it was supposed to be a wail but she might want to go back to the drawing board on that one. She let it roll though, she was hollering like she was at somebody's funeral. I halfway expected her to say, "Lord, take me, take me now!" I laughed. I heard Maya, trying to cover up the fact that she was crying too, but she did a piss poor job of hiding it, because when she finally spoke again, she could barely get the words out, "Th-th-th thank you Je-sus!"

HUSTLE GAME 16

AFTER another hour or so on the phone with the "two live crew", I got a beep, checked the screen and saw that it was Mr. Davis; I remembered I'd never returned his call from earlier. I told the girls I had to call him back, but we made plans to get together later in the week. Maya agreed to stay longer than her normal five hours tomorrow at work to cover for me; you never know what the peanut gallery is up to over at Globalnomics. I am the youngest VP; not to mention the only African American female, so, let's just say, I have a big ass bull's eye on my back. But what they don't know is, Nikki Pearson may be a lot of things, but scared damn show ain't one of them. As soon as I got promoted to my new position two years ago, I realized I was in the big league now and Mama Dearest always taught me ain't nobody going to look out for me, but me! So, what did I do...I fired my assistant.

Cindy looked and acted liked Malibu Barbie, but I knew her type. That heifer was not clueless by a long shot. Shit, if the trailer park didn't teach you anything else, it taught you how to hustle, just like the damn projects! Hell, that's the only way to survive... And game recognize game. No, Cindy might not have had the education and experience that I have, but word around the office was that she had one helluva blowjob. And THAT, mixed with street hustle was a bad combination in corporate America, cause some broad was always one blowjob away from the top! Setting women's liberation back decades. And I'll be damn if I was going to let some "Blowjob Barbie" come up in here and rain on my parade, Oh, no mam!

So, as soon as Maya and Jason decided Maya could go back to work part-time after the twins, I got rid of Cindy's ass. Who better to have watching your back, than someone that's got your back? Oh, and where they really fucked up at, is that no one at Globalnomics knows that Maya and I have been best friends for years and that Maya is more capable than I am of doing my job. Shit, my girl graduated summa cum laude of our class at Spelman, then got her MBA from Georgia State, summa cum laude, again! Not to mention, while Cindy's ass was growing up in the trailer park, learning how to hustle and I was growing up in the projects, learning how to hustle, Maya's ass was growing up in the hood, and all our hustle combined can't trump hood hustle! She just wanted to spend more time with her girls than in the boardroom. It's so funny sometimes, because Maya is always so professional, "Ms. Pearson this, Ms. Pearson that...but as soon as my door closes and we're alone, it's "Bitch this and Bitch that," because that's how friends are. Like mama used to say," what they don't know won't hurt them." Sometimes, I can just hear her voice ringing in my head, "You don't shit where you eat!" In other words, you keep all your business out of the work place cause that's what feed your ass. The only thing they know about my personal business up in that joint is this black bitch is getting paid! And when I get paid...Maya gets paid! There's not a bonus check I get, that my girl, Maya, don't get hers off the top.

PRINCIPLES 17

HEADING up 285 to Alpharetta, I am absolutely dreading going home. Although, I had booked my room for two nights, after I got off the phone with Jermaine, I didn't have shit to do, so I figured I may as well go home to make sure Steven's selfish ass didn't have his tired ass friends all up in my shit.

Sure enough, when I let the garage door up, that bastard wasn't even home. "Why do I do this shit?" I asked myself out loud. We're not lovers, hell, we're not even friends, I thought to myself as I entered through the garage and headed inside. "OH, HELL NAWl!" was all I could say as I climbed the steps from my sunken den and saw all those dirty dishes still all over my kitchen island. "I tell you what, " I said, reaching into my purse to get my phone, "I might not be his lover, and I might not even be his damn friend, but I know good and damn well I ain't ever going to be his fucking maid!"

"What's up, Babe?" He answered…on the fourth ring. Hmmm.

"What's up, Babe, my ass!" Screaming to the top of my lungs, "You got 'bout five whole minutes to get your nasty ass back over here and clean up my got-damn kitchen. This don't make no kinda sense, with your nasty ass!" Hanging up in his face, I stomped my way up the stairs. I was so pissed; tears were streaming down my face.

Just then the phone rang, "What!" I screamed so loud into the receiver, I scared my own damn self.

"He-he-llo, Nikki," Jermaine stammered. "Is everything okay?"

"Oh, I'm sorry, Jermaine. Everything is fine, " I whispered."

"Did I catch you at a bad time?" "If so, I can call you back some other time."

"Actually, you may be just what the doctor ordered!" oh. Shit, why did I just say that? "I mean, talking about Chelsea makes me feel better. Have you spoken to her today?"

"Well, that's actually the reason why I called. I called my mom when you and I got off the phone earlier and I told her you'd agreed to be in Chelsea's life. She was ecstatic. Instead of bringing Chelsea home next weekend, she can bring her home this weekend." I let out a light gasp. "Nikki, would you like to meet your daughter this weekend?"

"Oh, my God, Yes!" "I would love to meet her this weekend. Thank you, thank you so much, Jermaine!" I yelled, as I jumped up and down holding my heart, tears streaming down my face.

Chuckling, Jermaine's baritone voice once again filled the line, "Okay, okay...so that's a yes! I will give you a call later in the week and we can work out the particulars, okay."

"Sounds like a plan, talk to you soon." We hung up.

No sooner than I hung up the phone, I heard Steven coming up the stairs, I hadn't even heard him come in. "You know," he said, as he walked up to me, waving his finger in my face. "I'm sick and tired of your ass trying to handle me like I'm your bitch. If you think you can talk to me like one of your little flunkies down at your job, well, bitch, you got another thing coming!" Then smooched me in my face causing my head to snap back.

While, I am never at a loss for words, this bastard had me speechless. I just stood there, I literally could not move. I couldn't breathe, I couldn't talk...I couldn't do shit. It was like I was having an outer body experience, yet I could feel myself getting pissed. I know damn well that bastard did not just put his hands on me and I know he did not just call me a bitch! Oh, I got his bitch.

That coward was still walking around raising hell, like a bitch, like he had lost his damn mind. And I just watched. He's going on and on about how I had his friends clowning him. Fuck you and your friends I thought. Once I was able to move, I casually walked over to my bed, sat down and crossed my legs. He was still going on. I opened my cell that was still in my hand and pressed 911.

"911, what's your emergency?" I held the cell with my neck as I reached inside my nightstand drawer. He was still going.

"My name is Nicolette Pearson." He was still going.

"Hello, Ms. Pearson, what is your emergency?" I pulled out the 9mm revolver I kept for security purposes. Oh, he wasn't saying shit now.

"You have five minutes to get here before I kill this bastard, starting now." I said then hung up the phone as casually as I had picked it up. I reached over to the clock on my bedside table and turned the timer on 5:00 minutes. Now who's stuck, he didn't move an inch.

I took the safety off the revolver, never taking my eyes off the clock 4:49, 4:48...

He just stood there, scared shitless. That's a coward for you. Who's the bitch now, 3:45, 3:44, 3:43...I closed my eyes and softly recited my favorite scripture, "Lord, I confess my sins," 2:34, 2:33, "please be faithful and just," 2:20, 2:19 "to forgive me my sins," 1:58, 1:57 "and cleanse me from all unrighteousness." I opened my eyes and looked him dead in the eyes, 1:15; 1:14

"Drop the gun, mam" I heard an officer yell. Hell, I never even heard them come in.

Never taking my eyes off Steven's pussy ass, I laid the gun on the bed; stood up and walked over to the officer and said, "Perfect timing." That officer rushed over to where Steven was and the female officer outside the door grabbed my hands and pulled me into the guest room.

I could hear Steven in the next room saying, "That

crazy bitch tried to kill me!" The officer was trying to calm him, but of course, just like any other bitch ass nigga, he was hella-bad now that he had some protection. Listen to him in there acting just like them project hoes from back in the day, they would talk cash money shit when they were with their little click, but catch them hoes by themselves and it was like they were playing 1-2-3 still mouse. You couldn't pay their ass to say something!

The female officer said, "Ms. Pearson, what happened here tonight?" I recounted the events that led up to this moment. I was calm and respectful. "Ms. Pearson, did you threaten to shoot him?"

"Actually, no. I called 9-1-1 and told them if you all were not here in five minutes I was going to kill the bastard. I have yet to open my mouth to him since he came through the door. I never pointed the gun at him, I just took it out of the nightstand, took it off safety, closed my eyes and confessed my sins."

"Mam, would you actually have killed him because he called you a bitch and pushed you in your face?"

"No mam," I said, looking her dead in the eyes. "I was going to kill him for the principle of it."

The Aftermath   18

AFTER the officers finished their report and made sure my firearm was registered, they watched as Steven packed up some of his things and cleaned my damn kitchen. Once he had pulled out my driveway, the female officer looked at me and said, "Ms. Pearson, enjoy the rest of your evening and stay out of trouble," with a smirk on her lips. She then winked her eye, nodded her head and turned and walked away. With all the abused women they see on a daily basis, it must have been rather refreshing for her to finally see a woman put a stop to that shit before it even got a chance to start good. If I hadn't did anything this time, next time it would have been a full shove, then a slap, a punch, a kick and so on. Oh, hell nawl...not your girl, my own daddy ain't never hit me!

I went back upstairs; hit the play button on my surround sound system and the sultry voice of Alicia Keys filled the house..."*Cause a real man knows a real women when he sees her. And a real woman knows a real man ain't shame to please her and a real man knows a real woman always comes first...*" sitting in my bubble bath, I thought, "Lord, please let my daughter grow up and know her worth."

That night, I slept more peaceful than I could ever remember.

When I woke up the next morning, I instinctively

reached over to rub Steven's baldhead like I have done every morning for the past year. Then it hit me, he's gone. A wave of sorrow came over me, but was I really mourning Steven or was I just scared to be alone. Feeling a little melancholy, I headed down stairs to find something to make me feel better, Pecan Praline Ice cream. As I reached in the drawer to get a spoon, I laughed out loud at Steven's childish ass. He'd put the big ass cooking spoons in the drawer with the eating utensils last night just for the hell of it. "Nigga, the joke is on you," I said aloud. " Trying to be bad for your boys, now you ain't got no damn where to lay your head. I'm done with your selfish ass and you STILL had to wash them damn dishes!" His childish ass had just made my day and he didn't even know it. Shit, I needed that laugh. I was just about to miss his punk ass too! Humph...like mama used to say, "How could you miss something that you never had?"

I grabbed one of those big ass spoons and waved it in the air like a magic wand, "Poof...Bitch, be gone," I said laughingly and took me a big scoop of heaven...pecan praline.

After calling my girls and telling them about Steven's tired ass, I was even more rejuvenated. Those heifers had me on the phone killing myself laughing at Steven. Normally, I would have been offended, but, shit, it is what it is. If I am honest with myself, this shit has been over! We were just co-existing. Freaking, roommates at best!

I was just about to go get on the treadmill and do a

couple of miles when my cell rang. "Hellllll-ooo," I practically swooned into the phone.

"Well, I see someone is in a good mood today," Jermaine's laughter was almost contagious coming through the line.

Giggling like a school-girl, "Well, Mr. Davis, I must admit...Life is Good."

"Oh really." he said laughing. "I'm so happy for you then, Ms. Pearson. Congratulations! Seriously though, what time do you get off today? I was hoping you and I could get together to discuss how we're going to handle your meeting with Chelsea, since this is a fragile situation."

"Well actually, I played hooky today, so I'm sitting on my couch as we speak, finishing off the remains of some pecan praline ice cream," I said.

"Hooky, huh? Aren't you a little old for that?"

"One thing I've learned in this life of mine, Mr. Davis, is that you are never too old to put yourself first."

"Hmmm, damn, I had no idea you were that deep," he said laughingly, "and I would have to unequivocally agree with you!"

" Hey, I'm not much in the mood for going out this evening, but why don't you drop by and we can come up with a game plan," I said.

"Are you sure that's not a problem?" He asked. I don't want to invade your privacy."

"Since you have already told me your mother was a true southern belle, I know she would be appalled at you for questioning a woman's integrity. If I invited you over, that means you are welcome, besides we're practically family."

"Okay, if you say it's cool, I would love to come over. Is now good or would you like for me to wait for Steven to get home, so maybe we can all sit down and hash this out? "

I was taken aback for a minute; I forgot we had discussed Steven the night we talked on the phone all night. "No, now is just fine, let me give you the address to put in your GPS."

"Nikki, are you sure I should come over when he's not there? I'm a man and I know how territorial us men can be; especially about other men being in our homes when we're not there and I certainly don't want me and the brotha to get off on a wrong foot...in an already sticky situation. I just don't want any prob-----."

"Jermaine!" I yelled into the phone laughing, "Are you going to write my address down or not?"

"Okay, okay," he chuckled. "What's the address?"

"4-1-2-4...This-Is-My-Damn-House, Alpharetta, GA 30004", I said as serious as a heart attack.

The thunderous laughter that shattered my line made me laugh even harder. "Girl, you are crazy! Now, I see where Chelsea gets her sense of humor and her smart ass mouth."

"Well, what can I say?" I said, doing my best J.J Evans impersonation. After a couple of more laughs, I gave him my address and he was on his way. I ran upstairs, two stairs at a time, snatched the silk scarf off my head, and grabbed my electric toothbrush. I looked in the mirror and grabbed my MAC eyeliner and put on just a hint to add some color to my pale face. After applying some Vaseline to my lips, I threw on one of my Auburn University t-shirts and a pair of walking shorts and headed back downstairs. Shayla would have me committed for this ensemble but what the hell, it wasn't a date; we were discussing our daughter.

When the doorbell rang, it startled me. I had been reading last month's edition of Essence Magazine and lost track of time. The surround sound was now blasting Monica's, "Angel of Mine," and I was completely lost in the lyrics. When I opened the door, my breath got caught in my throat, then Florida Evans took over that little voice in my head again, "Dammnnn, Dammnnn, Dammnnn." "Hey, how are you?" I managed to get out. "I hope you didn't have trouble finding me?"

"Actually, my GPS brought me straight here, and that's saying something in this city. Can I come in?"

"Oh, my bad, my bad," I said, giggling. Lord, I hope he

didn't see me checking him out, I thought in my head. I'm so embarrassed. "Right this way, can I get you anything to drink?" Coffee, tea or me...what the fuck! Lord, help me get Mama Dearest out my damn head, I thought. "I've got some lemonade, sweet tea and bottled water or some beer or Moscato if you are in the mood for something a little stronger."

"Thanks, a beer is good, if you don't mind." The sensual sounds of Babyface's, "When can I see you Again" was filling the airways. As I handed him his beer, I could see him vibing to the classic hit. "Come on this way and have a sit." As I took a seat on the opposite couch, I reached for the remote and turned the music down.

"You guys have a beautiful home here and I love the view," he said as he looked out the picturesque window. It was such a beautiful day; the slight breeze had prompted me to open the glass door panels all the way and let the outside in. It had been forever since I'd sat down in the sunken den and enjoyed the view, times like these made me glad I'd worked so hard.

"Thanks, "I said softly. "To be honest, I work so much that I rarely get time to appreciate it. This was the one big purchase I made when I got my promotion to VP. I figured it was the least I could do for myself." Starring out into the wooded acres beyond the pool and fire pit, I suddenly felt sad.

Sensing my mood change, Jermaine thoughtfully raised his beer bottle, " Well, I salute you on a job well done, my sistah. I, for one, am proud of what you have accomplished in such a short time. Salute" I smiled. Then with a tone of seriousness, he said, "Nikki, I don't know you that well, but from what I know, you deserve this and so much more. And I know you have regrets, we all do, but just be thankful that God has saw fit to give you a second chance with Chelsea, a lot of people don't get that."

Laughing lightly, "Well, Mr. Davis, I had no idea you were a mind reader, too! Cheers to your many abilities!" I said and teasingly held up my glass to toast. Depression diverted.

We sat and chatted for a while making small talk, then we got on the subject of Chelsea. We decided to meet up at Piedmont Park and go on a picnic. The plan was for me to take it slow, just spend some time with her as a friend of her father's first, before we spring the biological mother fact on her. We both agreed that was the best approach.

We were actually having a really good time, just talking, getting to know one another. I had laid back on the love seat and was downing my third glass of wine and Jermaine was lying back on the sofa nursing his fourth beer. You would think we had known each other all our lives. Our banter was easy and unpretentious, perhaps because other than Maya and Shayla, he knew more about me than anyone else I know. That was quiet ironic, considering a week ago I couldn't pick him out of a line up. As he reminded me a few minutes ago, I couldn't even pick him out at Pappadeaux! We laughed about how long we both sat out there wasting time, waiting for the other to get there. His excuse was that he could never see my face from where he was sitting. He swears that he would have known immediately if he had seen my face because Chelsea looks just like me. I killed his theory when I told him this sandy ass hair should have been a dead giveaway, since she and I both share that as well. My defense was that I was looking for a couple, so I won that battle easily. I was in the middle of telling Jermaine how I met Shayla, when the doorbell rang. Walking to the door, I just assumed it was Mr. Smith from across the street, with his nosy ass, trying to figure out what was going on last night. Opening the door wide, I stopped mid-sentence, "What are you doing here?"

"Nikki, we need to talk," said Steven. "What happened last night shouldn't have happened," he said. I could smell the alcohol on him as he tried brushing past me.

"Hold up!" I said, gabbing him by the arm. "We don't have anything else to talk about and now is not a good time."

"What the fuck you mean, now is not a good time?" Trying to peep around the corner, "Who the fuck you got in my house?" Lord, what he had to say that for cause all hell broke loose.

"Your house, your house? Nigga, please, you ain't paid the first damn mortgage payment since you been here and your name damn sure ain't on shit here! Ain't shit here yours, including me! Now, get the fuck out and don't come back to MY house again!"

"Bitch, I ain't going no fucking where!"

"Bitch!" I screamed. "I know the fuck you didn't!" I hauled back and slapped the shit out of him. Just as he drew his fist back, I heard Jermaine's voice, "Man, I really wouldn't do that if I were you." Oh, Jermaine. I had forgotten all about him. Steven's punk ass was shocked as hell. The look on his face was priceless.

"And who's gonna stop me?" Steven said looking Jermaine dead in the eyes.

Jermaine's voice didn't quiver, "Oh, I'm not going to stop you. As a matter of fact, the way I'm feeling right now, I WANT your punk ass to hit her, cause that one lick is going to fuck up the rest of your life, Partna! I promise you that!" I was shocked by how cold and calculated Jermaine's voice sounded, he meant what the fuck he said and obviously Steven's punk ass knew it too because he dropped his damn hand with the quickness.

Then he looked back down at me and started whining like a bitch, "Babe, why you doing this to us? That's why you put me out? You fucking this nigga?" I have never been so fucking embarrassed, but more for Steven's whining ass than myself. I was thinking, "Damn, Nigga, Man up...don't be whining in front of another nigga, shit.... you making me look bad.

"Steven, please leave, it's over."

"Baby, please...don't do..."

Jermaine must have got tired of his punk ass whining too, because he cut his ass off mid-sentence. "Partna, she said leave! Now are you gonna leave on your own or am I gonna have to make you?" Taking, a few steps closer, his eyes were smoldering, affixed on Steven, and the muscle in his right jaw was quenching. I put my hand on his chest to shop him.

"Nikki, who the fuck is this nigga?"

" He's...He's my Baby's Daddy."

"What the fuck!" The look Steven gave me was of pure hate and disgust. "So, that's why your ass walking around here throwing up and shit, cause you done let some mutha-fucker big you?" Throwing his hands up while backing out the door, he said to Jermaine, "Oh, you can have the ho, Partna, I don't want her trick ass!"

Jermaine grabbed the knob and slammed the door as hard as he could. He turned around and leaned back against the door and looked at me, as I stood there with my head down. "So, you never told him about Chelsea?"

I looked up at him and shook my head "No."

ALL NIGHTER 19

PUSHING himself up off the door, Jermaine walked up to me and lifted my chin, "Are you okay?" I nodded my head up and down. With that, he grabbed my hand and led me back down to the den and gestured for me to sit. After he topped my wine glass off, he went to the kitchen and grabbed another beer out of the fridge. At this very moment the only thing I could think about was what it would feel like if I could taste those juicy lips of his. Standing at 6'5, roughly 235 pounds, he still moved around my home with the grace and agility of a skilled dancer, but by the way those jeans hung slightly off his hips and his Timberlands drug as he walked, he possessed the swagger of the toughest thug on the block. Damn, what a combination! When he came back in the room, stood over me, kicked off his Tims, looked down at me, licked his lips and said adamantly, "Start talking." I came all over myself.

After I was able to contain myself from the orgasm I'd just had from merely looking at this man. I gave him the filtered version of my life. I told him how I'd just found out I was pregnant the day my boyfriend and I broke up about another cheating incident. I went on to tell him how I'd originally planned on keeping my baby. I told him the filtered version of what happened when I went home to Macon to tell my mama I was pregnant and ask for help, careful, not to say too much. As difficult as it was, I tried to tell him what my life was like growing up with Mama

Dearest and my on again-off again, good for nothing daddy. I wanted him to understand why leaving my baby with them while I returned to school was not an option and how not retuning to school was not an option either, because statistics showed I would have ended up just like mama; uneducated, barely making ends meet or on welfare, in those same damn projects. And that's just not the life I wanted for my child. Adoption was the only logical option I had to try to give my child a better life.

I went on to tell him how Shayla and Maya stepped up to the plate and how I will forever be indebted to them. I remember so vividly, that Wednesday afternoon after Mama got off her soapbox in her hen house, I ran to my room crying because I knew then and there that I could not subject my baby to such an upbringing. I called Shayla crying and she told me not to worry that she would take care of everything. She asked me did I have any gas money to come back to school and I told her no. She told me not to worry about that either, she'll take care of everything.

"About 8:30 that night, I heard Mama Dearest yelling my name. I don't know why she always felt like she had to yell, we stayed in a three-bedroom project and the walls were paper-thin. Hell, that's how I knew for sure that Ms. Johnson had been fucking both of those married men for years. If my bedroom walls could talk, they would have ran her no-good ass right up out of Macon. Five babies with five different daddies, and the verdict was still out on two of them, and she had the audacity to try to give somebody some damn advice." Jermaine hollered in laughter at that. Now, looking back and having made it out...that was some funny shit. "Anyway, when I got in the living room, there was Mr. D, Shayla's dad. "Hey, Hon." he said, and kissed me on the forehead like he's been doing since I was eight years old. He handed me an envelope, "Shayla told me you were going back tomorrow because you had a test and to send this package by you. I said, "No problem, Mr. D." We bid our goodbyes, while Mama and some of her hen house crew waited on the front stoop for him to come back out, so they could get their flirt on. Not one of them actually thought Mr. D. would cheat on his wife with their tired asses but I guess it just made them feel good to try because they'd been doing it for years. I just laughed at their ridiculousness, I told Jermaine. Hell, the hens in the hen house were the reason I called Mr. D., Mr. D. After mama's first encounter with him at the school, of course she went home and told the hens about the fine ass man she'd met at my school. Since I was so young, my mama wouldn't let them used the "d-word" when I was around," I was saying but Jermaine cut me off.

"What's the "d-word, "Damn"?" He asked, killing himself laughing.

I hit him in the head playfully, from where he was sitting on the floor down by feet. "You play too much, are you going to let me finish my story or not?"

"Okay, okay, I'm sorry. Go ahead, I just needed to know what the "d-word was!" He threw his head back in another fit of laughter.

"Anyway, all that day they talked nonstop about how they knew that was some good "D" and what they would do with that "D" and how they bet his wife don't even know how to ride that "D". So the next morning when I saw him, it just flew out of my mouth, "Good morning, Mr. D.!" He was actually bent over now, holding his stomach in bouts of hysteria. I couldn't help but laugh myself.

"Hold up, hold up, I got one question," he said, still laughing uncontrollably.

I cocked my head to the side and looked at him, "What?" Cause I already knew this was going to be some foolishness.

"Seriously, though," he said, trying hard to contain his self, "Does Shayla have any idea why you call her pops, Mr. D.?"

"If you knew my mama, you wouldn't even have to ask me that! Shayla and I were inseparable. She would spend her summer sitting in the beauty shop listening to those hens cackling while I washed hair. I used to tell her she didn't have to, that I would catch up with her after my mama let me off, but she actually liked sitting up in there listening to that shit. I hated it! Once we got a little older, the ladies in the shop called her Shayla "D"...cause she CUM from that good "D"! She thought it was funny...but then again, you got to know Shayla, too! He thought this was hilarious.

"Back to the story that matters, "I said. "I won't ever finish with you around. Anyways, Mr. D's package for

Shayla had three hundred dollars in there. Which he thought he was sending to get books for next semester. I put gas in my car and went back to school. That weekend, we went apartment hunting in Lithonia, so we would be unlikely to run into anyone from school once I started showing. We all finished out the rest of the semester in our dorm room together. Shayla nor Maya did not go to school for the Summer semester that year but I did because I knew I wasn't going to be able to go during the Fall because I would be showing and I did not want to get behind. All of us got jobs for the summer, well, let me rephrase that...we all got jobs, but Maya and me actually kept ours. Shayla said she was too fine to work...and ironically, she still says the same damn thing." He laughed. "We paid our bills and put the rest in the OBF. I was so depressed, that was the worst time in my life. They did everything they knew to comfort me. Not only was I dealing with a broken heart but I was also having a baby without a daddy or my mama.

"Hold up, so you never told ole boy you was pregnant?"

I dropped my head, "Nope."

"Damn, that's messed up." "Okay, what is the "OBF"?"

"My bad, I'm so used to saying it...it's the "Our Baby Fund," we started it at Bank of America once we got jobs, and we each contributed whatever we could afford to it every month."

"Okay, back to homeboy. Was he your dude, for real,

for real or was you like his...jump-off?"

I shrugged my shoulders, "Honestly, I don't even know anymore. From what I know now, he was doing so many, who knows what I was. Let me put it this way, cause you're a man, you probably know more than I do. I was SUPPOSED to be his girl, and I was the only person he would be with in public. I don't know if that made me his girl or just a public fool. I don't know and I don't care, "I said sadly.

He laid his head back in my lap and looked up at me and said, "Baby, it's alright, he was young, that's what young men do, they think with their dicks. It does not make you any less of a woman, okay?" Then he licked his lips. Damn.

"Okay, Dr. Phil," I said and burst out laughing, trying to take my focus off those juicy ass lips. I'm going to hell.

"Didn't he try to get you back though?"

"Yeah, he tried calling but I wouldn't talk to him. He came by my mom's when I was there those two weeks, but I wouldn't come out my room. I guess after a while, he said fuck it. He didn't want me anyway, he just didn't want nobody else to have me."

Shaking his head and chuckling a little, "Shit, you can't blame the man for that!" I pushed his head off my knee as hard as I could. "I'm just saying," he said laughing and throwing his hands up.

I continued, "After summer semester, I withdrew from school and the only time I went outside of our apartment was to go to my doctor's appointments. Shayla and Maya took care of everything.

"So what made you change your mind about keeping her?"

"I compared statistics about kids given up for adoption versus kids raised by unwed, teen-aged parents and once I was honest with myself, I knew I couldn't do it by myself and I didn't have a family support system. And although Shayla and Maya were willing, I could not allow them to give up their lives to take care of my responsibility. So, once I'd made up my mind, I was about seven and a half months, I broke down and called Mr. D."

"Wow, Mr. D., really?"

"Yeah, when I called I actually chickened out though, instead of telling him, I just made small talk, which wasn't that strange because I would call him from time to time, because him and Mrs. Daniels were more like parents to me than my own.

"So, what happened?" He was sitting up now like a little kid waiting on a cookie.

"Well, we hung up and I laid on the couch and cried myself to sleep. I was awakened by a knock at the door about and hour and a half later. Naturally, I just assumed it was Shayla that did not have her key. She would do that from time to time, if she didn't want to carry a purse and she said keys sticking out in her pocket was a "no, no." She was to fly for that. And we never had any visitors because of my situation. So, I just flung the door open without checking to see who it was and there was Mr. D. He took one look at me and just opened up his arms, I fell into arms and cried like a baby. He led me back to the couch were I had been laying and just rocked me like I was his own child. I love that man. Once I was able to talk, he and I discussed everything. He answered all the questions I had about adoption and told me he would take care of everything."

"So, why did he come, if he didn't think your call was strange?"

"Actually, it never dawned on me that day to ask him why he came, I was just thankful he was there. But a few weeks later while he sat in the doctor's office with me, I asked him what made him come to Atlanta that day. He told me that a father knows when something is wrong with their child and he knew something wasn't right just by the sound of my voice. But when I went on chatting like nothing was wrong, he dismissed his initial thought. But then he said, when I said "Bye, Mr. Daniels," at the end of our conversation, he knew for sure something was wrong."

"Huh, I'm lost," he said, looking puzzled.

"You're slow too, I see," I laughed. "I just got done telling you that he's my, Mr. D. and always had been. He knew something was seriously wrong because I had never once called him Mr. Daniels. So, he said, he jumped in his car right then because he knew I needed him."

"Ahhhh man, that's some deep shit right there," he said.

"Umm...do you realize it's 4am," I looked down and asked Jermaine.

"Ahhh, man, I knew it was late but I had no idea it was that late." Laying his head back on my knee again he said, "I guess I better go," and licked those lips.

Releasing the breath caught in my throat, I licked my lips, "You don't have to," as I gazed into the sexiest hazel eyes I have ever seen.

FAMILY AFFAIR 20

FRIDAY evening, as Maya and I got off the elevators in the lobby and waved our goodbyes for the weekend, I reflected back on how this week had been the first time in forever that I haven't had to battle with depression. All I have had this week were happy thoughts, as my nieces Khia and Shia would say when they saw someone crying, "Think happy thoughts, TeTe," they would say and reach to wipe my tears. Those little girls were so sweet but being around them always made me think about what I had given up. Not anymore, nothing but happy thoughts from now on.

By the time I was able to navigate through the crowded downtown streets, Maya had already taken MARTA and was waiting by the curb at Peachtree and Spring Street for me to pick her up. This had become our ritual on days we were hanging out after work. We would wave goodbye at the elevators in the middle of the spacious lobby for everyone to see. Then I would give the valet my ticket and she would head for the MARTA station across the street. Two Marta stops later, she would get off and wait for me at the corner, hop in and off we'd go. Several times we'd considered not taking it this far, but I could always here mama's voice in the back of my mind saying, "Chile, you never let your right hand know what your left hand is doing." I smiled at the thought.

As we zoomed through the streets of HOTLANATA,

headed to interstate 75, Maya caught me up on the latest office gossip. We strategized about a couple of accounts and laughed at Samuels' stubby ass for getting caught with his pants down, literally. Word on the street was, Pricilla, his ugly ass wife, walked in the conference room late one evening when he was supposed to be working late and his secretary, the infamous Cindy, was on her knees earning her promotion. I told you that trick had some hustle game, that's why I hustled her little ass right up out my space. She did okay for herself though; cause she ended up as Samuels's secretary and that rat bastard was CEO.

As Maya recanted the story she'd gotten directly from Leon, Samuels's gay assistant, I thought I would die from laughing so hard. According to Leon, when Ms. Thang came switching into the office that Thursday afternoon basically dismissing him, oh, he had had enough. Leon said it was bad enough the cunt walked around like she was Princess Di, waving her hand and expecting everybody to jump, but when that heifer told him to drop what he was doing and go down and fetch her a latte, she had lost her ever lasting mind. Maya did her hilarious Leon impersonation, with the three snaps up, "Oh, hell nawl!" Maya said, "Hon-ney, Ms. Leon said SHE makes $100, 000 a year, SHE sits on the board of two global companies, SHE don't fetch no mutha-fucking coffee!" I literally screamed that shit was so funny! Continuing on with the saga, Maya didn't skip a beat, "Ms. Leon swears he did not call Cruella Deville, I mean Pricilla Samuels, to come down to the office that afternoon, but I know Ms.

Leon, and although she probably didn't do it herself, she made damn sure it got done. The last person you wanted to piss off was a weave wearing sissy! Because they ain't scared of shit and they don't play by no damn rules. We haven't been able to get a crack out of Samuels' ass all week! Cruella's got his ass by the balls and word is... Cindy didn't even get a severance package on her way out the door. Now, that shit was gangster.

As we turned into The Fish Market's parking lot, we both burst out laughing. There stood Shayla on the porch, surround by a throng of men. In pure Shayla fashion, she was working it, with her huge sunglasses and a scarf around her head. She was giving calculated tosses of the hair, slight hand throwing and touching her chest as she gave a stellar performance, in true Marilyn style! Shaking my head as I handed the keys to the valet, "Some things never change." Maya and I both laughed.

As she saw us approaching, she really turned it on, "Darlings," she drawled, "what on earth took you so long?" These idiots were hanging on to her every word but we didn't even stop and entertain that foolishness. With a toss of her hand, she bid them farewell and headed inside behind us. I laughed until I cried.

We were in that restaurant for fours but it only seemed liked 15 minutes. When we get together it's as if nothing or no one exists around us. We actually have to meet in public places, that way we'll have no other choice but to go home. Maya told us all about her plans for her annual Father's Day Extravaganza at her in-laws. While

Maya and her crew calls it a Bar-B-Que; Shayla and I renamed it an EXTRA-vaganza because Jason's family is so damn big, every year they have at least ten extras added to their clan. Shit, Shayla says they multiply like fucking roaches. What's even funnier is that all nine of Jason's brothers are fine as hell but Shayla hasn't fucked the first one of them. She swears those fine, country bunkins literally scare the shit out of her. When we finally got a chance to meet them all at Jason and Maya's anniversary party at his parents' South Georgia farm...Shayla was ecstatic.

I remember it like it was yesterday. I was getting some lemonade out of a cooler and Shayla walked up and whispered in my ear, " Do you see this shit?" " Every one of these brothas can get it, hell, even the damn daddy!" I had to grab a hold of the table to keep from falling to the floor, while she walked away in pure Marylyn form like she hadn't said shit! About an hour or so later, I looked over at her because I just knew she would be ready to go because all those damn mosquitoes, gnats and flies were probably running her ass crazy, but no, that ho threw me the fucking thumbs up sign. She was surround by all the brothers and the cousins and loving every minute. The hussy had the nerve to shoot me a text, talking about "Girl, I am happier than a faggot with a bag of dicks!" I literally hollered, everybody looked at me like I had lost my ever-lasting mind.

One of Jason's sisters, Monique, leaned over to me and nodded in Shayla's direction, "Tell your girl, trust me, that ain't what she want!" And we both laughed so hard until I cried. I never got around to relaying the message to her though, because about two hours, forty-two kids and twenty-six baby mama's later, she caught the damn hint..."that ain't what she want!"

She walked over to me and said, "Girllll, get me the fuck outta here, these country ass niggas are deadly!" Jason's sister, Monique, and I cracked our sides laughing at her. Until this day, she swears those are the only men she's ever been scared of and she will not let us leave her alone with none of them. She told their mama, Mrs. Stella, affectionately called Ma Dukes, "I don't mean no harm but it ain't nothing I can do with neither one of their fine asses but look, cause I can see them talking the drawers right off my ass and have me stuck down here in Mayberry with a house full of kids and my nose wide open. No, thank you..."and she wasn't even performing that time.

We were given the menu items we were supposed to bring. It 's funny because we go through this every year, the same argument, I get mad because I actually have to bring dishes, Peach Cobbler and Banana Pudding but all Shayla's diva-fied ass has to bring is cups, plates, napkins and the cutlery sets. Every year I would say, "Now, what grown ass woman is asked to bring paper products to every damn function?" And every year, Maya would end the argument by saying, "Do you really want to eat anything she cooks?" Enough said. We'd laugh at the thought. .

Being out with my girls took my mind off meeting my

daughter for the first time tomorrow. I have been so nervous all week but Jermaine assured me that Chelsea would love me, to just be myself. He was being so sweet, trying to put me more at ease. Every morning, he would send me a different picture to my cell of some momentous occasion in her life and tell me about it. And every evening, he would send me either recordings on his cell that he had of her, so I could see her face and hear her voice before I went to sleep. He was so thoughtful. I told the girls all about it, they were just as happy as I was. Tomorrow could not come soon enough.

CHELSEA 21

I was a nervous wreck; I have probably worn a hole in my carpet, pacing back in forth in front of the bay window overlooking my cobblestone driveway. That reminds me, I've got to find a new lawn service to keep up my yard. Bitch Ass Steven had a friend who owned a lawn company and he would pay him to maintain it every other week but now dude said he can't do my lawn anymore. Screw him and his bitch ass friend, I thought. Just as I was about to start pacing again, I saw Jermaine's black Silverado pull into the driveway. All I could do is stand at the window with my hands over my mouth as I watched the sandy haired, chubby face little girl, jump down out of the truck's cab. MY sandy haired, chubby face little girl. As she began running up the sidewalk, Jermaine must have yelled for her to stop because she obediently turned and skipped back to where he was and lovingly grabbed his hand.

As they made their way up the walkway, I was finally able to will my feet to move from where I had been glued. Wiping the tears from eyes, I opened the door, just as Chelsea was about to reach for the doorbell. She looked up at me, eyes wide in awe, like a deer in headlights. I fell in love. Impulsively, I reached down and started tickling her in her stomach and the sound that came out of her throat was infectious. In between gurgles of laughter, she sputtered out, "Daddy, help me, Daddy." But he was laughing just as hard as she was. Once I finally stopped, I hugged her to my leg until she was able to catch her breath and contain herself. When she looked up at me grinning from ear to ear, I said, "Hi, Chelsea, I'm Nikki. It's so nice to finally met you."

"Hi, Mizz. Nikki, I'm Chelsea," then she burst into a fit of laughter and flung her tiny hands over her mouth, "oh you already know that!" That tickled us all.

"Would you all like to come inside for a minute, while I grab the picnic basket?" I couldn't take my eyes off her. She strolled on inside like Dorothy on the yellow brick road and began looking around in amazement. As Jermaine walked in behind her, he gently squeezed my hand; my eyes were still on her.

"Mizz. Nikki, your house is soooooo prrrrrrretttty," she said in awe. "When I grow up I want to have a pretty house like this," she said, while twirling herself around in the middle of the room looking at everything. Her dad said she was quite perceptive for her age. Yep, she's mine.

I kneeled down and met her eye to eye, then took her hands in mine, "You, young lady," I said, tapping her on the bridge of her nose, the nose so much like mine and my mother's, "will have an even better house than this when you grow up!" Her eyes lit up, my heart melted.

"Would you like to see the rest of the house, I asked her?"

"Yes, yes, yes", she started screaming, jumping up and down.

Laughing I said, "Well, ask your dad if it's okay."

She ran over to Jermaine and grabbed him around one leg, "Please, Daddy, Can I?" He nodded his head yes and off to the races we went.

She grabbed my hand and led me from room to room like it was her house. She wanted to know what everything was. Once we came back down stairs, I noticed Jermaine had taken the liberty of packing up all our picnic essentials and was sitting on the chaise by the door. "Ladies, come on, why don't you?"

We both threw up one finger at the same time and said, "One more minute." She and I looked at each other and burst out laughing. Jermaine just shook his head and threw his hands in the air laughing, and said, "Lord, help me!"

Once we had finally completed our downstairs tour, five minutes later, out the door we went. I cannot ever remember being this happy in my life.

I could not believe how lucky I was as I lay back on the blanket and watched as Chelsea and her dad raced over to the slide. She is a bag full of energy but I love every minute of it. With her around, I can stop my gym membership because keeping up with her is definitely cardio, weight training and the way she had me trying to teach her how to turn cart wills, I think we covered yoga as well. As Chelsea joined in another game of duck-duck goose with the other kids she had befriended, Jermaine ran over and took a much-needed break. Flopping down onto the blanket, in pure exhaustion, he said, "Are you okay, she's quite the ball of energy, huh?"

Laughing aloud, " You can say that again, you should have prepared me to get ready for a triathlon, but I love it. While, I must admit, I have never spent a lot of time outdoors; I am having the time of my life right now. She is everything you said she was and so much more. Thank you"

"Thank me for what?" he asked.

"For my child," I whispered with a voice cracking on the verge on of tears.

"No," he hit me on the tip of my nose, "Not today, only happy thoughts." How sweet I thought as I smiled up at him, he made me think about Shia and Khia, I cannot wait for them to meet Chelsea.

Jermaine and I lay on the blanket and watched as Chelsea played with the other kids for hours, she was in heaven. "I'm so glad she is getting a chance to get out and meet other kids, " Jermaine said, more to himself than anyone.

"Do you miss New Orleans?" I asked.

"Sure, I miss it," he said sounding distant. "You know, I was born and raised there so, I guess, it's a very big part of who I am. I know, a lot of people feel a strong connection to where they're from, but when they choose to move away and relocate for whatever the reason, it doesn't resonate the same as having been forced to move away from all that you know. You know what I mean?" I nodded my head. "Having to stand by and watch everything you've worked for and that your fore-fathers before you worked for just wash away is one of the most helpless feelings anyone could have. As I gathered my family together that day after the levies broke, I felt like I was less than a man. I couldn't do a damn thing to stop what was happening to my family." My heart ached for him. I listened intently, also mourning his loss, "I had to literally drag my mother out of her home, the home were she was raised, her mother was raised and she had raised all of her kids. I can still hear her cries sometimes at night, it was so heart wrenching, coming from a place deep within because she was already mourning the loss of her past. People didn't understand, all they saw was that we should have felt blessed for making it out when hundreds of lives were lost, but they couldn't see that part of us did die that day. That's why so many people committed suicide in the days that followed, because the devastation was too much to bear." Suddenly, jumping to his feet, he shouted, "Happy thoughts!" but not before I saw him wipe away the fresh tears. He grabbed me by the hand and pulled me up in one quick swoop, "Come on lady, let's go play with our daughter!"

As soon as we pulled away from the park good, Chelsea was a fast asleep. We rode alone in silence, both deep in our own thoughts...happy ones. As we got closer to my house, I broke the silence, looking over at the beautiful man that had made all my dreams come true, "Jermaine, this has been the best day of my life."

Rubbing my hand, "Don't worry kiddo, there are more to come." He flashed the most amazing smile, and the electricity bolt returned.

"Would it be too much too soon if you and Chelsea came over tomorrow?"

"I would love nothing better." I told him goodnight and hopped out of the truck's cab. He waited until I was inside of the house before he pulled away. I stood in the window and watched the truck until the taillights were completely out of view. I cried, happy tears.

LIFE IS GOOD 22

AS I was getting out of the shower, my cell pone rang from over on my nightstand. "Hello," I answered.

"Mizz. Nikki, I want to see you now!" My hands flew to my mouth to stop the escape of the sob that was caught in my chest.

"Well, what are you waiting for my dear, tell your dad to bring you to see me right now!"

"Daddy, Mizz. Nikki said you better bring me to see her right now!" She yelled.

A second later, Jermaine's silky voice came through the line, "Oh, really, Mizz. Nikki said I better! Is that right?" We both laughed. Giggling he said, "I'm sorry, but I could not contain her any longer, she's been trying to get me to bring her to see you since 8am. Every five minutes she'd say, "Daaaadddddy, I want Mizzzzz. Nikkkkk-kkkkkiiiii!" I laughed at his impersonation of Chelsea.

"I wish you had called because I've been up since 7:30 thinking about her and hoping it wasn't just a hoax yesterday and she might not like me today."

"Baby, I don't think you have anything to worry about, she's a pretty good judge of character." Did he just call me, Baby? I thought.

An hour later, Jermaine and Chelsea were pulling into

my driveway, and this time Jermaine could not stop Chelsea from running up to the door and straight into my arms. Giving me a big hug, she said, "Mizz. Nikki, can we play dress up?"

"Oh, don't look at me, I'm not playing dress up!" Besides I got other things I need to do." Off to my room we went, Chelsea leading the way like she had been born and raised in this house.

The first thing she wanted to do was put on makeup, no surprise there. As I was applying the makeup to her face I told her, " Chelsea, as you get older, don't forget you don't need makeup to make you beautiful, you are beautiful just the way you are."

She shook her head, "Yes, Mizz. Nikki." Then it was my turn, she was now the stylist and I was the client. Which got me to thinking, I hope she hasn't already been taken to her first Spa Day; maybe she and I can still create some "first" memories together. "Mizz. Nikki, Don't I need music for my clients to sing to?" This child was so smart.

"You are absolutely right, my dear, but let's check to make sure it won't disturb your dad if we turn the music on." I called out to Jermaine but did not get an answer. "Let's go find your dad, Sweetheart." She grabbed my hand and we trotted downstairs but we did not see Jermaine anywhere.

"Maybe Daddy's playing hide and seek, Mizz. Nikki. He's really good at that."

I laughed, but then we heard the sound of a lawnmower outside, we headed towards the noise and peeped out of the den window, and there was Jermaine pushing a lawnmower. We opened the back door and went to investigate further. He waved at us from across the yard and then headed in our direction. When he was near, he released the handle on the mower, turning off the loud noise. Shaking my head I asked, "Where on earth did you get a lawnmower?"

"I stopped by the Lowes up the street and grabbed it on the way here."

"Oh, my, God, you didn't have to do that, Jermaine. I was going to find a new lawn service provider tomorrow."

"Why should you have to do that?" "I'm here, it needs to be done and I'm not doing anything else, especially make-over's," as he pointed to our faces laughing. All I could do is shake my head; this man was full of surprises. "Gwon back inside nie' woman, dis here's man's work," he said in the worst cowboy impersonation I've ever heard.

Obediently, Chelsea and I turned to go back inside, but not before she asked the question I knew was coming sooner or later. "Mizz. Nikki, can we please get in your pool?" Laughing aloud, I took her hand and we skipped on inside.

"We'll see," is all I said. As we began our appointment, this time with the music blasted because we clearly were not going to disturb Jermaine. We danced and sang along with the latest radio hits. After my make-up had been so expertly applied by Chelsea she grabbed my brush and unraveled the braid going down the center of my head and began taking long, soft strokes. In the tiniest voice I've ever heard from her, "Mizz. Nikki, is my hair going to grow long and thick like yours too?"

"Sure baby, your hair is going to grow long and thick just like mine."

"Mizz. Nikki, am I going to be pretty like you when I grow up too?"

"Chelsea, you're already pretty and you're going to be even prettier as you grow up, just wait, you'll see." She threw her arms around my neck from where she was standing behind me and said, "I love you, Mizz. Nikki!" I could not contain my emotions, I cried and held onto her until she was ready to try on heels. I know now, I am going to have to solicit Shayla's help the older Chelsea gets because she is going to be a bonafide diva, I thought.

After another hour or so, I told Chelsea we need to go down stairs and fix a little lunch because her father was going to be hungry after he is done with the yard work. I peeped outside and to my surprise, he was actually weed eating now. He must've spent a fortune in Lowes; I'll have to remind myself to write him a check.

Chelsea and I went downstairs and got busy in the kitchen. I must admit that it felt good to actually be cooking again. I used to enjoy things like this but once I realized Steven's trifling ass didn't even appreciate the effort, I stopped. What was the point of working 10-12 hours a day, then coming home and slaving over a hot stove and the bastard was too selfish to show up at a decent time to eat it. After a while, I didn't give a damn if he ate or not.

I taught Chelsea how to make fresh squeezed lemonade; she then helped me prepare homemade spaghetti sauce and noodles. She took great pride in going through the spice rack and adding different herbs and tasting it afterwards and telling me what it needed more of. She was actually good at it, especially for a six year old. She said she helps her grandmother cook a lot back in New Orleans. After we had our lunch together, we set out to do the preparations for our dinner, baked beans, pasta salad and baked potatoes. The steaks were already marinating and I had also prepared one of my infamous peach cobblers that morning as well.

Funny, I just took it for granted that they were going to stay over that long. If I had to grab Jermaine around his leg and beg like Chelsea, I wasn't taking no for an answer.

Jermaine, knocked on the window and startled the both of us, we giggled, "Let the garage door up," he said while wiping perspiration from his face.

"I'll do it, I'll do it, " Chelsea jumped off the stool and was off to the races, knowing exactly where to go and what to do. She's so smart I thought. As Jermaine stored the mower and the lawn equipment neatly in the garage, I gathered him two bottles of bottled water and met him at the door. Handing it to him, he flashed me a dazzling smile to show his appreciation. In one day, he'd taken more liberty around here than Steven's sorry ass ever had. Every two weeks I had to remind him to call Carlos' crew to come do the yard. You would think he would see that the damn grass needed to be cut; he looked at the same shit, every damn day, just like I did. Hell, if it were up to him, the grass would have grown taller than the damn house itself. But, you can bet your ass I never had to tell him when it was time to cut his damn hair, which was an everyday ritual.

I sure as hell didn't have to remind him to wash that damn Tahoe that he loved so much. Every Friday like clockwork he dropped it off at Sip & Soak on his lunch break, but do you think he ever bothered worrying about either of my vehicles being washed. And unlike Jermaine, that bastard would have never considered getting in the yard and cutting the grass or washing the car his damn self, with his pretty ass. I can't speak for most women, but I for one, love a manly man. One that sees shit needs to be done and does it. I can't stand to see grown ass men standing on the side of the road, waiting on AAA to come change their freaking tires. Really, Dude? The AAA operators ought to hang up on their punk asses when they call in with that bullshit. Some shit you just don't do!

Chelsea was showing Jermaine to the guest room so he could shower and get ready for lunch when my cell rang. As soon as I answered, Maya went on a tirade, "Listen Heifer, this shit is getting old now! I gave your ass a pass for a while but half of the day has gone by and we ain't heard shit from you about how yesterday went. I think

Steven's inconsiderate ass done rubbed off on you!" All I could do is stand there with my mouth dropped open.

"Maya, honey, you're right and I am soooooo sorry. It went absolutely fantastic! Yesterday was honestly the best day of my life...but today is coming in a close second."

"What's happened today?"

"Girl, even though Jermaine and I had already made plans to get together today, Chelsea called me first thing this morning and told me she was ready to see me now!"

Maya laughed, "Damn! Sounds like your mother."

"I know, right, but in a good way! So, they have been here since around 11. We've played dress up, had makeovers and ripped the runway. I'll tell you, she's going to loooooove Shayla. We just finished making lunch; she's upstairs now showing her dad to the guest room so he can wash up because he just finished cutting my grass. I'm going to beg her dad to stay until this evening so we can get in the pool and throw some steaks on the grill. You got to see the swimsuits I bought for her this morning.

"Swimsuits?" Damn, girl, how many did you buy?"

"Four," I said softly. "I know, I know, but they were all so cute, I couldn't make my mind up, so I just got them all."

Laughing so hard, "I'm sure she is not going to have

any objections; especially if she has an hint of Shayla's personality. I am soooooooo happy for you, Nikki, and I can't wait to meet her."

"Thanks Maya. Thanks for everything, I love you girl."

"Right back at you, Chick! I'm not going to hold you up; you enjoy every moment. Bye, Love."

And with that the line went dead. I called out for Chelsea, who ran to the top of the stairs, "Baby are you okay?"

"Yes, mam," I'm just putting your shoes back where they go, thank you for letting me wear them Mizz. Nikki." I smiled, thinking...he has raised her to be thoughtful too.

You would never guess that he's not her biological father because they share such similar traits. Mama used to say, "Well, if you feed em' long enough, they'll look like you," when she used to be talking about Ms. Jones' kids, but mama might've been wrong on that one, cause I still don't know who all their daddies are. I laughed to myself.

After lunch, we all played UNO. After several rounds of that, Chelsea wanted to play Trouble, which she beat us in twice. Then she ran and picked out a book from the collection I'd brought this morning at Wal-Mart. "Daddy, please read to me and Mizz. Nikki."

He looked at me with those eyes, which seemed to twinkle with mischief, "Mizz. Nikki," licking his lips, "Would you like me to read to you?" He licked his lips again. DAMN! I looked him in the eyes and nodded my head. Feeling the burning sensation between my legs getting hotter and hotter, I barely heard him as he began the story…"Once upon a time there was this girl called Nancy No-Size. Nancy was not short, Nancy was not tall; Nancy was no size at all…" In my lap, Chelsea, was mesmerized by the story, which wasn't hard because her dad made sure he emphasized in the right places, he showed the pictures, hell I was captivated too…but not by Nancy's No-sized ass.

By the time Jermaine had finished the story, Chelsea was winding down and so were Jermaine and I. He gathered her off of me and I went upstairs and got some pillows and blankets and made us a pallet on the floor and the three of us took a nap. It was so peaceful.

DAMN SHAME 23

THE sound of the ringing doorbell pulled me out of a deep sleep. I'm not sure how long we had been asleep but we obviously needed the rest. I jumped up to try to get to the door before it woke Chelsea, but Jermaine groggily said it was okay because she needed to wake up anyway or else she wouldn't sleep tonight. So, I got up from the floor and left him laying lazily there with his hands behind his head, I know that sun had him wore out.

As I peeped out the door I prayed silently, "Lord, please don't be Steven's punk ass, ain't nobody got time for that shit today." But as I peeped out the peephole all I could see was the palm of someone's hand blocking it. Laughing, I reached for the doorknob; I should have known Maya's nosey ass would pull a stunt like this. I opened the door with my hands on my hips, "What are you doing here..." but before I could finish my sentence good, she'd shoved one of the twins in my face who was saying "TeTe," yeah that trick knew how to get me. "Heyyyyyy, TeTe's Babies," I said as I reached for the other twin too and they began to plant kisses on my cheeks, my heart swelled. I looked at the peanut gallery, Maya, Shayla and Jason, standing there with covered dishes and bags, looking pitiful like I might not let them in. Laughing at their antics, I said," Come on in," and moved aside so they could enter. Jason came in first, then those heifers hugged me and Shayla whispered, "I promise we'll be on our best behavior, we won't let on to her."

Maya looked at me at said, "Sorry, Nik, but she's our baby too. We'll be good."

And as if on queue, Jermaine rounded the corner carrying a still groggy Chelsea. They both said in unison, "DAYMMMMNNNNNNNN!" and then threw their hands over their mouths and looked at me.

Jason burst out laughing and walked towards Jermaine, I just shook my head and looked at them, " Be good? Yeah right!"

At least somebody was acting like they had some damn sense, Jason was still shaking his head when he got to Jermaine, "What's up, Dog, I'm Jason...please forgive the "Two live Crew" they act like that ain't never seen a fine brother before," and popped his collar. We all laughed.

These hoes were still holding hands, making faces at each other like the man wasn't standing here. So, I attempted introductions, but Shayla, who just two minutes ago was going to behave herself, slung Maya's hand down and put on the sexiest stroll I have ever seen and made her way over to Jermaine, then held her hand up for him to kiss it. REALLY BITCH. "Hi, I'm..."

"Shayla," he said, finishing for her. And he laughingly kissed her hand.

Then he reached out his hand to shake Maya's, but

instead she pulled him into an embrace. "Excuse her and I'm so happy to finally meet you, I've heard so much about you."

"Not enough, apparently," Shayla said, looking him up and down like a juicy steak.

"And you must be Chelsea?" Maya asked.

Chelsea giggled, "You already know my name?"

"Yes mam, we all do!" And we could not wait to meet Mizz. Nikki's new friend!" Chelsea looked over at me and smiled from ear to ear. "These are my girls, Shia and Khia, they wanted to come over and play with you. Would you like that?" I must admit, Maya got this mama shit down pat; she was a regular Susie homemaker!

Nodding her head "yes," Chelsea jumped down, ran over to me and hugged my legs as I put the girls down. She said, "Mizz. Nikki, they look just alike, like me and you!"

All of our heads snapped up, my eyes met Jermaine's, he said, "That's right, Chelsea, you are absolutely right!" And laughed, so we all nervously followed suit.

Oblivious to the nervous adults, Chelsea led Shia and Khia down to the toys she'd been playing with earlier.

As I headed toward the kitchen, I could feel all eyes on me. I opened the fridge to get Jermaine a beer and said, "Jason, is beer good for you, too? I asked as I handed Jermaine's beer to him.

"Sure, I never like to see a man drink alone," he hit Jermaine playfully in the chest and we all laughed.

"And what do ya'll heifers want?" Before she could get it out because she was already pointing to Jermaine, "To drink, Shayla, my God!" I said sounding all exasperated. Everybody laughed, except me.

"I'll get us some wine glasses down. Shayla, you uncork the bottles I brought," said Maya, trying to diffuse the situation quickly.

"Well, ya'll know where everything is, I need to go outside to clean the grill because I'm quite sure Steven didn't do it the last time he used it."

Jermaine smacked his mouth at the mention of Steven's name, then said, "Don't worry, I already cleaned it."

"You did?" "When did you do that?" I asked looking at Jermaine.

"I did it when I first went outside this morning before I cut grass. I saw that you had purchased some charcoal and lighter fluid so I figured you would be using it some time soon, so I checked to see if it was clean, it wasn't, so I cleaned it."

"I hope that's okay," he added.

"Hmmmm, that's perfectly fine! I hate doing that kind of stuff. Well, in that case, can you guys go get the grill ready and we'll get things together in here, then we can all hit the pool with the girls."

"Sounds like a plan, but let me get us one to go on," said Jermaine as he made his way over to the fridge, smirking at me the entire time. He grabbed two more beers, tossed another one over to Jason and headed out the door.

"Dammnnn!" They both yelled and high-fived each other! Then both of them turned their attention to me. I tried to start unpacking the items they'd brought to avoid the questioning stares. Shayla spoke up first, "So, when did we stop telling each other everything?" she whispered, careful not to let the girls overhear.

"That's a damn good question," said Maya through quenched teeth.

"I don't know what you're talking about, I have told ya'll everything. What the man looks like didn't have anything to do with the price of tea in China. Hell, I barely even noticed."

"Bitch, pleeze!" Maya said before I could barely even finish my sentence. "Ain't no way in the hell you didn't notice all-that-man! Shiiiiiit, when he came around that corner, I forgot my fucking husband was in the damn room," she whispered. We giggled at that, because that reaction was very uncharacteristic of Maya.

Shayla chimed in, "Now, I have seen some fine men in my life. Shit, I have had some fine men in my life. But that, out there," she said pointing out back, "Is one of the finest men I've ever fucking seen!"

"We can tell," both Maya and I said. "And remember you promised to behave yourself," I warned.

"I know, I know. I promise I'm going to behave. Hell, he don't want my ass anyway!" She said and strolled over to tap me on the nose to emphasize her point." And if you know, what I know...you better give him what he wants!"

Laughing, she walked back over to Maya and they clinked their glasses and made a mock salute to me.

"Whatever man, ya'll don't know what you're talking about, that man ain't even looked at me like that."

"Ho, you've been knowing me a long time, and you know I'm an expert at this kinda shit. And you also know, there ain't but two kinds of men that don't want me... a gay man and a man whose nose is already open for another bitch." She waved her hand in the air for affect, "And...ain't a damn thing gay about that brotha out there!"

I gazed in the direction Shayla was pointing just as Jermaine glimpsed up from pouring the charcoal on the grill. When our eyes met, he flashed a bright smile...and I damn near came on myself...again. That man was truly one of the most beautiful creatures I 'd ever laid eyes on too. Standing around 6'5 or 6'6, tall, athletically built; like a pro ball player, just the way I like them. About 235 pounds, give or take a few, with some of the smoothest, darkest mahogany skin I have ever seen. The silky hair on his face and head was even darker; it was a complete contrast against the rich mahogany of his skin. Deep caramel coated eyes, with a cute little nose. The damn man was perfect, literally.

After the girls and I had completed our kitchen duties or should I say, after Maya and I had completed our duties because Shayla didn't do a damn thing but whine, so we hurried and dismissed her ass. She did however; fulfill her auntie roles with the girls by giving them all a makeover to die for. Then once she had them decked to the nines, she dressed them in their bathing suits and taught them how they should strut when they become Ms. America. It was so cute, the girls were having the time of their life, and Shayla was enjoying having their full attention.

This day was even more perfect than the day before, it was amazing how Jermaine fit right in with us, as if he had been knowing us all of his life. The two-live crew, or even Jason, for that matter, had never responded to Steven this way. We swam, ate, laughed and played with the twins and Chelsea until they passed out on a chaise lounge, both girls laying facing Chelsea, like she was the joy of their world. It was priceless. I can never remember being this content in all my days. Jason broke into my daydream, " As much as I am enjoying myself, I think we need to get our little supermodels to bed."

"That's his code ya'll, he thinks they're sleeping hard enough for him to get him some tonight! " Everyone laughed at Maya's candidness; including Jason, who was quick to point out how although she was talking shit, she was packing up the girls' bags ninety to nothing trying to get home to get it.

Jermaine carried Chelsea as we walked everyone to the door and said our goodnights. Jason and Jermaine had really hit it off with one another. I think they had talked about every sport ever invented in the history of sports; Jermaine had even agreed to join Jason and some of his friends at the Hawk's post-season playoff game this Friday. Then he suddenly turned to me, " Nikki, I'm sorry for making plans without discussing them with you...but do you think you will be able to watch Chelsea for me while I go to the game with the fellas?"

Of course all eyes were on me, including the caramel set that were now causing my panties to melt away from skin. Stuttering I said, "Yo-You don't have to apologize, I will love to watch Chelsea any time!" Unexpectedly, he then put his free arm around my shoulder and pulled me to him affectionately. Now, not only were all eyes on me, all eyes were on us!

And Shayla loved every minute of it, " Ahhh, shit, Jason, looks like you ain't the only one who might get lucky tonight!" Everyone laughed, except for me, who was beet red at this point, which only gave my girls even more ammunition for later. Damn!

LOSS FOR WORDS 24

ONCE both cars had backed out of the driveway, we headed back inside. Jermaine laid Chelsea down on the couch and headed out back. I stood and watched intently as he secured the pool and equipment in their proper places, locked the gates and turned off the lights. It's just something about a man that takes initiative, I thought. "Yeah, it's something about his ass all right; he's sexy as hell," said the other voice in my head.

Once he had locked and secured the back door and the garage door, he turned to me, "Nikki, I had a wonderful time, in fact, this was the most fun I've had since coming here four years ago and I'm sure, the same goes for Chelsea. Thank you so much for allowing us to meet your friends, I really like them. Is there anything else you need me to help you with before we leave?"

Suddenly, my heart ached, I hated for this day to end, but I just shook my head "No". "If it's okay with you, can I get the rest of Chelsea's things another time?" He asked. Still unable to force a sound from my throat, I simply nodded "Yes". When he grabbed his keys, I held my breath. When he walked over to where Chelsea lay, I felt a teardrop fall. When he reached down to pick Chelsea up, I yelled, "Don't!" Startled, he quickly turned to look at me for clarification and what he saw was pure distraught. I've always prided myself in not being a typical emotional woman but at this moment all my pride was out the window. "Babe, what's wrong?" He asked as he rushed over and caressed my tear stricken face. By now, my words were pure formulations that existed only in my head because I could not get out one, single word. My sobs just continued to worsen. He pulled me closer, pleading with his eyes and his mouth to get me to tell him what was wrong but at this point I could barely breath I was crying so hard. He pulled me tight into his embrace, promising that everything would be all right, stroking my hair, he begged me not to cry anymore.

Just as more uncontrollable sobs sprang to life; I heard Chelsea yell, "Mommy, don't cry!

Then she woozily jumped off the couch and ran into my arms, saying, "Please, don't cry, Mommy, don't cry!" As we hugged her tight, Jermaine and I just stared into each other eyes for what seemed liked hours. While my sobs slowly subsided, Chelsea drifted back off into oblivion. Slowly, Jermaine lifted Chelsea from my arms, grabbed my hand and led me over to the pallet we'd left on the floor from earlier. He laid Chelsea down and then gestured for me to lie next to her. I held Chelsea tight as I watched her father as he proceeded throughout the house, turning off lights and straightening things up as he went along. Thoughtfully, he walked into the restroom and turned the light on, then cracked the door ever so slightly, leaving the room soaked in a soft amber glow. As the sound of Maxwell softly filled the room, Jermaine nestled down on the pallet and pulled me close. Twice in a lifetime, I was at a loss for words.

DUH??? 25

"MIZZ. Nikki, Mizz. Nikki, " I heard Chelsea whisper early the next morning, as she tried to keep from waking her dad, whose breath I could slightly feel upon my neck. With her face almost pressed up against mine, she whispered, "Mizz. Nikki, are you alright?"

Reaching up, caressing both sides of her face, my heart bordering on bypass with emotion, I said, "Yes, Precious, I'm perfectly fine. As long as I've got you, I'm perfectly fine." Seemingly satisfied, she nestled her body back into my embrace, where we both happily fell into another deep slumber.

When the smell of bacon assertively hit my nose, I turned to see the dreamiest caramel coated eyes gazing affectionately down at me. " Hey, sleepy head, I tried waking you but when that failed, I got creative and went with a more conventional route for a country girl like you...the smell of bacon works every time," he said laughing.

"Ah ke-ke-ke!" I said, imitating, his early morning antics. " Where is Chelsea?" I asked.

"She's taking a bubble bath before breakfast, since neither of us had a chance to clean up properly last night. How are you feeling this morning?"

Dropping my head to avoid eye contact, I said, " I'm fine, Jermaine, thank you for being so considerate last night and not leaving me alone like that. I don't know what came over me."

"Nikki," he said reaching for my hand, pulling me to my feet and against his rock hard abs, "The pleasure was all mine."

As we stared into each other's eyes, lost in yearning, a small voice said, "Daddy are you going to kiss Mizz. Nikki?" Giggling with childish delight.

We could not help but to giggle along with her, still holding my hand, Jermaine led me to the couch as he beckoned for Chelsea to join us. As we sat down, he pulled Chelsea on his knee. " Sweetheart," he said to her, "we need to talk."

"I'm sorry Daddy," she said. "I didn't mean to."

"Sorry for what?" He asked her with grave concern etching his voice.

Dropping her head, she began to cry. "What is it, Baby?" He asked. She looked from her dad, to me, then back to her dad, like she was terrified.

Sensing her pain, I said, "It's okay, honey. What are you afraid of?"

"That you still don't want to be my mommy!" she blurted out with a flood of tears.

At that very moment, my heart felt like someone had inserted a sword and twisted it as hard as they could. I looked into Jermaine's eyes for guidance and he nodded his head as he rocked Chelsea ferociously. "Chelsea, dear," I said as I pulled her up from her dad's shoulder to look at me, "There is nothing I want more in the world than to be your mommy, I've always wanted to be your mommy!" She looked at me with a state of confusion in her eyes and it pained me that I was the one that put it there.

In a voice barely above a whisper she said, " Well, why did you give me away?"

"I know it's hard for you to understand, but I really thought I was doing the best thing for you because I was so young and I could not take care of you the way your dad could." Tears were now streaming down all of our faces.

"Well, why did you try to keep it a secret from me?" She asked with all earnest.

Jermaine spoke up, "Honey, no one was trying to keep it a secret from you. We just did not know the best way to break the news to you, so I asked Nikki to wait until I thought you were ready. Do you understand?" He asked, looking at Chelsea for confirmation.

"But Daddy," she whined, " I been ready! I always wanted my mommy!" At that, she leapt out of his arms and onto my lap, planting kisses all over my face. We all laughed, feeling relieved.

Jermaine stretched his arms on the back of the couch and instinctively I fell back in them, holding Chelsea close. He then, planted kisses atop both our heads, as he rubbed my shoulders. "Sweetheart," he asked, as he tilted Chelsea's chin to look up at him, "How did you know Nikki was your mother?"

"Duh!" She said and opened both her hands..."I look just like her!" "Duh!"

NEW BEGINNINGS 26

EVERY day that followed was totally and utterly priceless. I actually took a leave of absence from my job so that I could spend as much time with Chelsea as possible. Jermaine would drop her off with me in the mornings before he went to work, and by the time he got off, Chelsea and I would have him a nice, hot, home cooked meal waiting on him. Some evenings after dinner, we would play Uno, Monopoly or take a dive in the pool, as a family. On the weekends, we tore up Atlanta; from Six Flags to Stone Mountain to The Martin Luther King, Jr. Memorial, nothing was off limits.

One Saturday evening, after spending the day with Maya, Jason and the twins, after grilling in the back yard, Chelsea begged me to go home with her TeTe Maya, as she so affectionately called her. "Please, Mommy, may I go, please. I want to go home with TeTe." It was so cute, we all laughed. Looking over at Jermaine for confirmation, he said, "Nikki, we're in this together, you don't need my permission to make decisions about our daughter, that's called parenting. I stand behind any decision you make where Chelsea is concerned."

Nodding in confirmation and the utmost respect, I said, "Thank you." Then I looked down at Chelsea and said, "Sure honey, why not!" With that, she, with the twins right on her foot took off upstairs to grab the bag she had packed to stay with me that night.

"Lord, " I said, "I think I may be a little jealous, three hours ago, she was looking forward to staying here with me tonight, and now she's leaving me for her "TeTe", playfully rolling my eyes in Maya's direction. Everyone rolled in hysterics.

Jermaine hugged me and said teasingly, "It's okay, you poor baby! If you want, Daddy will stay here and play with you." Maya and Jason got a good laugh at my expense as I pushed him away from me, still pouting.

As they were getting ready to leave, Chelsea hugged her dad first, then ran into my arms and said, "I love you, Mommy!" My heart literally stopped beating at that very moment. Maya joined in our embrace with tears of her own in her eyes.

Surprisingly, Jason broke up the moment, "All right Oprah and Gayle break this sensitive shit up and let's go," while pulling Maya and me apart. Jermaine thought that was hysterical, I looked at him and lovingly rolled my eyes cause if we were Oprah and Gayle, his ass was Dr. damn Phil cause he had tears in his eyes too! Just as they turned to leave, Jason turned around and hugged me and said, "I hope you know, Nik, I am really happy for you!" Releasing me, then pushing me in the forehead, he said "But I'm still pissed cause ya'll heifers could have told me after all these years," he said looking over at Maya. "I slick feel some type a way, you just don't sprang that kinda shit on a brotha." We all laughed at his candidness.

Maya snapped her neck and said, "While you looking

over here at me, you better hope Nikki ain't on her way to her nightstand, you remember what happened to the last nigga that pushed her!" Killing herself laughing, she started imitating me loading my gun and calling 9-1-1. Jermaine and Jason were on their knees laughing, and I must admit, that shit was funny!

Like usual, Jermaine and I set into our normal nightly routine, tidying the house back up. We were so comfortable with one another; you would think we'd known each other all our lives. While I was putting the dishes away in the dishwasher, he began sweeping the rich, mahogany hardwood floors, which ironically was the same shade as his skin tone and that thought sent sensations throughout my body. This was actually our first time being alone since the first night he came over and all the feelings I felt that night were coming back in waves. Much deeper waves.

Trying to keep my composure until he got the hell out of dodge, I thought I'd bring up a safe subject. "So, how's your mother?"

Without looking up, seemingly deep in thought, he said, "She's good actually. She said she'll be up here next weekend. Umm, I asked Maya if it was okay if she came with us to the father's day cook-out, but I suppose I should have asked you first." Looking at me he asked, "Would you like to meet my mother?"

Surprised by his hesitancy, I said, "Sure, why would you think that I don't want to meet your mother?"

"It's not that, it's just that I'm not sure just how much of our lives you want to intertwine, because you haven't mentioned introducing Chelsea to your own mother."

Damn. Where's this shit coming from I wondered? I turned to face him, leaning against the marble island, "Babe." Oh, shit I just called him Babe, I thought. "I would be nothing short of honored to meet your mother. That woman loved my daughter even when I couldn't! I have the utmost respect and gratitude to her for that! Not to mention, she raised you, Chelsea's dad, who loves her unconditionally!" Lovingly, I said looking directly into his eyes; those sexy, caramel coated..."I owe your mother my life."

Smiling sheepishly, he walked over and pulled me into an embrace. So much for choosing a safe subject, I thought as I felt the moisture drip in the axis of my thighs. Damn, he smelled good as I inhaled the pure essence of masculinity. As he released me, he leaned down to kiss the top of my head at the same time I looked up at him. The gleam in his eyes suddenly transformed the caramel into dark, rich amber, smoldering in raw sex appeal. Without saying a word, he pulled me hard against his body; my breath caught in my throat at the feel of his hard erection pressing ferociously against my midsection and then his mouth passionately claimed mine. The electricity that had emanated in me since the first time I laid eyes on him, was now spurring from my soul. In one full swoop, he reached down and scooped me up. My legs instinctively wrapped around his waist, his mouth never left mine. Finally, he pulled back and said roughly, "Tell me if you want me to stop."

Momentarily, I was dazed; I couldn't even react. Then an overwhelming sense of urgency took over me and I reached up and pulled his lips back to mine and I could feel the earth tilt on its axis around me. This man, in this moment, is all I wanted. As if he could hear my thoughts, he sat me on the marble kitchen island, while his tongue continued to assault my senses. Ripping my shirt from my body, he leaned down and took my inflamed nipple into the depths of his hot mouth. Leaving a trail of kisses, he grasped the other nipple and affectionately showed his appreciation by suckling as if his life depended on it. Glorious sensations cursed through my body, as he inserted a finger under my skirt into the folds of my womanhood. Lost in his touch, nothing and no one existed at this moment but this man, this wonderfully virile man. As my vaginal walls exploded around his caress, he let out a moan of pure ecstasy, which sent chills through my body and rocked me to the core. As his fingers worked magically and rhythmically inside me, he pulled his mouth away from my breast and gazed longingly into my eyes and what he saw there unleashed a raw sensuality within him. He swept everything off the oversized island, pushed me down on my back and after removing his shorts and t-shirt, he climbed on top of me. Kissing me viciously, he masterfully pulled my skirt down the length of body, followed by my now soaked satin panties. With all his masculinity pressing against my walls, begging feverishly for acceptance, he pulled my breast once again into his liquidity mouth and assaulted my soul. Looking down into my eyes, "One last time, tell me if you want me to stop," he said gruffly.

Unable to articulate, I grabbed this head and pulled it down onto my swollen lips, my tongue begging him to continue on his quest. Removing his finger from the folds of my inner being, his mouth neglected mine and replaced the finger he had deep inside of me. As his tongue danced inside of my flower with the rhythm of a trained ballerina, I lost my connection to the world around us. My body was on fire and all I could think about is how much I want to please this man. Waves of pure ecstasy escaped my soul, never have I experienced the magnitude of pleasure that I am witnessing at this very moment. As his tongue dove deeper into my lagoon of womanhood, I called out his name in pure delight. Then when I thought I could take no more, his long, hard manhood consumed the depths of time as he entered me with a feverish passion. Magically, our bodies intertwined passionately and soared on a rhythmic voyage that transcended reality into the depths of time, and then we climaxed, together.

BABY BOY 27

NEVER in my life had I experienced lovemaking so raw and passionate at the same time. Lying sprawled all over the kitchen island, I honestly felt like I was Thanksgiving dinner, and he had gloriously devoured the fest that was me; and my palette had left him completely satisfied. Lifting his head from my shoulder, he asked, "Babe, are you okay?"

Finally able to speak, I said, "I'm more than okay." Which sent his dark features into a wide grin from ear to ear. With that, he gently rolled off me, then off the oversized island. When picking out the marble slabs with my contractor, I never knew that it would be used for such purposes, but I loved every damn minute of it. He carefully placed his strong arms underneath my still quivering body and lifted me gently, bringing his mouth down on mine, he supplied me with the most passionate kiss I've ever had and then carried me upstairs to my bedroom. There he laid me on my bed, as his eyes roamed over the length of my body, I slowly watched his penis as it became more engrossed and I promise that was the most beautiful sight in all of nature. With his smoldering amber eyes never leaving mine, he climbed on the bed and entered me swiftly and strongly. With every long, hard stoke, my senses escaped my mind, body and soul until once again, I succumbed to the depths of his fervor. Once he felt my muscles squeeze into submission, then and only then did he surrender to the passion that overtook us both. We fell asleep in each other's arms.

The next morning, I woke to sound of Jermaine's gentle snoring in my ear. Looking at his beautifully, chiseled features, I willed myself not to think about tomorrow, to just enjoy what we have right here and right now. With that thought, I decided to pamper him a little. Easing from under his arm and out the bed, I checked to make sure I had not disturbed him. I gingerly made my way out of my room and across the hall to the guest room so that I would not awake him. As I leaned against the sink, waiting for the water to warm up, my thoughts drifted back to last night's lovemaking session and I was ecstatic. Smelling his scent all over my body sent chills throughout my soul because I felt like I've waited all my life for this moment. Nothing had ever felt so real. Shaking my head in the bedroom mirror, I headed downstairs to fix a hearty breakfast.

As I headed back upstairs carrying a tray with all his favorites, I guess subconsciously, my mind had been taking inventory over the past few weeks, just for this moment. When I entered the room, he was laying back on the pillow, with his hands underneath his head, starring up at the ceiling. When he heard me come in, he looked over at me with the sexiest smile, "Good morning, Sexy."

Smiling shyly, thinking of all the positions he had me

in last night and how he had really laid it down, I replied, "Good morning, Mr. D.... I mean Jermaine!" He doubled over in laughter and I joined in. As I sat the tray at the edge of the king-sized bed, he grabbed my arm and pulled me to him, still laughing.

"Oh, so you think I got some good "D"?" He whispered sexily in my ear. All I could do was release a soft moan, as he put his tongue inside my ear and expertly moved it in and out, the same way he'd done on my clitoris the night before. With his finger, he moved back and forth over my nipple creating a field of friction through the silk nightgown I had on. "Thank you for bringing me something to eat," he whispered huskily and with that he scooped my body up, sat me on his face and proceeded to feast on the delicate folds of my pussy. I came over and over again, calling out his name with every climax. Sexy chocolate...

After he finally let me off the tongue ride of a lifetime, I was too spent to feed him breakfast in bed like I had intended to, I merely curled up in the fetal position and moaned. I simply watched as he devoured his breakfast feast. After finishing his second glass of freshly squeezed orange juice, he swatted me on my behind, teasingly saying, "Come on Babe; let me get some more!" The joke was on him though, because I slowly rolled over, never taking my eyes off of his, reached over and grabbed the surround sound remote from my nightstand, laid back down, still staring at him and as Destiny Child's, *Cater To You*," filled the airways, I spread my legs, and slowly inserted my finger into my pussy. In and out, one finger then two... He sat still, watching, mesmerized for as long as he could, but when I slowly took my fingers out, rolled them back up the length of my body and inserted them into my mouth one by one and began to suck them...he lost total control. The tray sitting on the bed went sprawling to the floor but neither he nor I even noticed, as he entered me hard and fast. All I could think as he yelled out my name in a passionate trilogy is..."humph, you better find somebody to play with!"

As we lay in bed talking later that afternoon, I suddenly remembered we had to go pick up Chelsea from Maya's but then he told me not to worry he had it all taken care of. He'd called Jason earlier and asked if Chelsea could stay the rest of the weekend. "Oh my God, what reason did you give Jason for asking such a request?" I asked, with my hands over my mouth, my heart beating wildly in my chest.

"Calm down, Baby! I didn't tell him anything and he did not ask. He just said they would be more than happy to keep their niece." Letting out a sigh of relief, I felt so much better. Feeling at ease I began to smile to myself.

As he got off the bed and headed towards the bathroom door with his firm muscular ass, he looked back at me and said, " but if I were you, I'd wipe that goofy ass grin off my face. Jason didn't ask any questions because he already knew the damn answer!" My face registered pure shock. "Hell, what grown ass man call and ask another grown ass man if he could babysit for a whole damn weekend, if ain't no ass involved?" Jeeze!" He thought it was hilarious, and then he had the nerve to do the "beat it up dance" like Jody from the movie "Baby Boy." I was flabbergasted as I threw a pillow at his ass. But as soon as I heard the shower come to life, I forgot all about Maya and Jason and what they would think, and went and joined him in the shower and let him beat it up again.

INSEPERABLE 28

AS we pulled up in front of Maya's and Jason's ranch style home, the girls sprang from the door like wild deer. Chelsea, with Shia and Khia on her heels, "Mommy, Daddy," she screamed. "Thank you so much for letting me stay with TeTe and Uncle Jason, we went to the fair and then we went to see Ma Dukes and Papa."

Jermaine looked at me, puzzled, I mouthed, "Jason's parents." Nodding, he listened to our daughter intently, "Daddy, I fed the goats, we rode horses, we jumped on the trampoline...I can't wait to go back this weekend." We all laughed at her excitement.

With Jermaine carrying Chelsea and me carrying the twins, we entered the house, where Maya and Jason sat on the couch looking at us like the cats that swallowed the canary, although, neither said anything and for Maya, that was a fucking first. As the girls made their way back to the twins' room; we all made small talk mostly focusing on Maya's Father's Day Extravaganza. Then the guys ushered us to quiet down as their attention turned to Sports Center's announcement of a major 3-way trade impending for the NFL. The only named that registered inside my head was Kevin Williams. I'm sure my face turned as white as a ghost, but the guys were hanging onto every single word of the reporter, so they didn't even notice. Maya, always able to think on her feet, jumped up and said, "Girl, come on here, these trifling

Negros done dismissed us for some damn football," and although she practically had to drag me to my feet, neither one of the men noticed.

As we went out back and sat under the gazebo, Maya said, "Honey, why have you not told that man yet?

All I could do is hunch my shoulders, "I don't know."

"Well, Nikki, I'm here to tell you that it's not going away. He's her father and you not telling Jermaine is not going to change that. It's obvious you two are getting closer and you don't want to start something with lies or secrets between you. Let me go on the record saying, you're playing with fire."

"You're right, but it's not that big of a deal. Kevin has moved on with his life and what he doesn't know, won't hurt him or Jermaine either, for that matter. I appreciate you Maya, but I'm going to have to do this my way. Telling Jermaine about Kevin will only complicate things."

Sounding more confident than I felt, I got up and headed back inside. Strolling over to Jermaine, I sat in his lap and gave him a deep, passionate kiss. Needless to say, I shocked the shit out of Maya, Jason and even Jermaine's ass. So much so, that neither man protested when I turned the television all the way off and brought up an entirely different conversation. We talked and laughed for hours before we finally got up to bid our farewells. As we were heading to the door, Maya eased up behind me and said, "Bitch, I see you learned quiet a bit from Shayla's ass over the years. And the Oscar goes to...." We doubled over in laughter, high-fives and all.

Listening to Chelsea chatter nonstop as we drove home was refreshing to Jermaine and myself. Our child was a happy, vibrant little girl, as it should be. Although, we'd had a glorious weekend, Jermaine and I had not discussed what our little interlude meant for us. Instead of beating around the bush, when we pulled up in my driveway, I decided I was taking my fate in my own hands. As Jermaine left the truck running and Chelsea jumped in my lap to tell me "Goodnight," I decided it was now or never. I was no longer taking what was given to me; I was taking what I wanted. I reached over and turned off the ignition, Jermaine looked puzzled. Then I told Chelsea to get her bag, she was staying here from now on. She jumped up in merriment but then the realization hit her and her face darkened. She then looked from me to her dad, then back to me. Not taking my eyes off his, I rubbed her head and said, "Don't worry, Honey. Your daddy is staying here too, from now on." With my heart beating a mile a minute, it seemed like an eternity, but then he leaned over and kissed me with more passion than ever before. Chelsea was so excited; she started clapping and leaned in a kissed us too. As he got out of the truck and came around to my side, I thought... mama always said, " Chile, ain't nobody gonna give you nothing in this world, if you want something, take it!" And as my family and I strolled into our home, I thought, my mama was a lot of things, but stupid damn sure wasn't one of them.

That night was heaven, after I had gotten Chelsea

ready for bed, we all settled down for a quick game of Uno. At this time, she filled us in on how she wanted to decorate her new room. She wanted her walls painted her four favorite colors, blue, red, pink and purple. Jermaine tried to explain to her that favorite meant she had to narrow it down to the one she like the most, but once our little Chelsea had her mind made up, there was no changing it. Mama Dearest at her best, I thought. Then it was off to bed for her. I lay in the bed beside her as Jermaine read her a bedtime story from her favorite book. Once, she had drifted off to sleep, her father and I kissed her goodnight once again, and exited her room quietly. At the door, he waited on me, placed his arm around me and we walked down the hallway to our bedroom. "Why, Mizz. Nikki, you are full of surprises if I must say so myself."

Giggling, I said, "Why "Mr. D" you don't even know the half, grabbing a handful of his "D" I pulled him hard against my body, stood on my toes and leaned up for him to grace me with those sexy lips. Ummmm, I can drown in the taste of this man I thought. With that, I pushed him away and went into the bathroom. Watching the hot water as it cascaded into the Jacuzzi tub, I thought about how my life had changed so drastically in a matter of weeks. My life no longer existed around my job; in fact, I don't care if I never work again. Steven's tired ass and the loneliness he brought along with him was a distant memory. My house was now a home, filled with love and laughter. I was finally complete.

As I headed back into the bedroom, I stopped at the

door to lovingly watch Jermaine lying shirtless at the foot of the bed, with the remote in his hand, dozing as Sports Center watched him. Then, Kevin's face flashed across the screen of the 60" Plasma adorning the wall and for a brief moment I felt a longing deep in the pit of my stomach. Shaking off my fear, I walked over to Jermaine, took the remote and turned to the Silky Soul music channel, kissed him on the cheek and told him to come join me. Like a little boy at Christmas time, he jumped to his feet as if he were never asleep. As I led him into the candle lit bathroom, I started undressing along the way. By the time we made it to the double vanity, I was completely naked. I turned to look at him, and then I reached out and slowly began undressing him. By the time I got to his boxers, Mr. D. was standing at full attention. Looking up at him all the time, I slowly removed his boxer shorts and in one swift move, I was on my knees and his glorious dick was inside the crevices of my warm mouth. As I slide his shaft in and out, I paid close and thorough attention to the throbbing head of his engrossed penis, as I suckled deeply where all the nerves were. His head was thrown back and there was nothing but moans of pure ecstasy as I pulled him in and out...I could probably do this shit every day, I thought as I feasted on his glorious dick. Hell, for this man, I know I could. His strong hands were entangled in my hair as he held on to the side of my face, crying out in pleasure, then as he began to jerk feverishly, he said, "Baby, I'm about to cum, I'm about to cum." In response, my jaws tightened even more around the long, hard shaft, as I sucked harder one last time, I felt his body tense and heard the sounds of unadulterated bliss before I felt the warm liquid ooze down my throat. As he pulled me from my knees, all he could muster was, "Damn!" Then he had me up against the bathroom wall, pounding inside me, flesh to flesh. As sweat caressed both our skins, his rich mahogany black and mine a creamy, blush, olive; we became one. Inseparable.

MAMA DEAREST 29

AS I lay in bed, watching Jermaine get ready for work , I said, "Honey, I think it's time I took Chelsea to meet my mother." He stopped mid-stride and turned to look at me.

"Are you sure you're ready to do that, Babe?" I don't want to rush you to do anything you're not ready to." He sat down on the bed next to me and took my hand.

Gazing into those eyes that I've grown to love, I touch the side of his cheek and said, "Honestly, it's past time. Now, that I've become a mother in every sense of the word, I realize that my mama really was not half as bad as I thought. While I did not agree with everything she did or said, her influence has been positive in my life. So, if you don't mind, Chelsea and I are going to drive to Macon and surprise her today."

Kissing me softly, he said, "Of course, I don't mind! If you need me to, I can get someone to cover for me and I can come with you."

"I appreciate that honey, you are always so

considerate, but this is something I have to do myself. I'll see you when we get back, okay." Nodding his head, he hugged me tight to his body, then gave me a kiss on the head and was out the door.

As we drove down 75 South, towards Macon, Chelsea asked a million questions about her grandmother. I told her about the good times in my childhood as Auntie Shayla and I grew up. I told her how funny her grandmother was and how she did not take any mess from anyone, except, maybe, my sorry ass daddy, but I thought it best to leave that part out. I didn't want to scar my precious baby for life.

As we got off on the Eisenhower exit, and headed in the direction of my mother's apartment, I thought it was best to call her to make sure she was home. Mother Dearest answered on the third ring, as usual. "Well, well, well, twice in one month, Chile, are you sick?" She laughed nervously.

"No, Mam. I'm not sick. What are you doing?"

"Well, I just finished curling my hair, you know that's been my Monday routine for as long as I can remember."

"Do you have company?" I asked.

"Chile, you know your daddy don't work on Mondays and I don't play having all them heifers around here when he's here. That's a no, no...you don't put shit past no ho." I laughed something serious; because once again, her insight was right on point. I wish I had listened back in college. "Chile, what do you want? What's with all these damn questions? You act like you with the IRS or something."

"Oh, nothing. I was just wondering did you get the package I sent you?"

"Nawl, Melvin ain't brought no package around here, when did you send it? Sometimes, I b'lieve he be in that bottle and gets my mail mixed up with Ms. Johnson's next door."

As we got out the car and walked up the walkway, I said, "Nawl, I don't believe you and Ms. Johnson are getting the same kind of packages delivered from Melvin."

She roared in laughter, "Chile, you 'shole right bout that!"

Laughingly I said, "No, I had this package hand delivered anyway, go check the front porch before one of Ms. Johnson's bad ass kids gets it."

Striking a nerve, she said, "I wish they would bring their dusty foots...AHHHHHHHHHHHHHH, WHAT THE HELL? What are you doing here?" She asked as she opened the screen door for me to come in.

"Mama, I came to bring you a package," with that I moved to the side. Clutching her heart, my mother let out a loud shriek. Her eyes instantly welled up with tears as she reached down and stroked Chelsea's face. Touching her hair, her eyes, her nose and finally she pulled her into a warm embrace. I had never seen my mother cry until this very moment. The always-strong woman, I called Mama Dearest, now seemed so fragile as she held onto the child for dear life. Leaving me standing there, she turned, still clutching a quiet Chelsea to her bosom and headed to the living room where my dad sat watching Andy Griffith. "Cleve, Cleve...I told you, I told you!" My Daddy looked up to see what all the commotion was about, but when my mother sat Chelsea down and turned her to face him; he just looked from her to me, then back to her. Standing, he walked faster than I'd ever seen him move and stood in front of Chelsea and said, "Oh, Barbara, you were right!" And starting laughing as loud as I've ever heard him without a fifth of Jack in his hands.

He picked Chelsea up and spun her around, crying happy tears. Mama Dearest joined in the tirade; Chelsea was all giggles, yelling, "Faster, Granddaddy, faster!"

I literally sank to the floor, not sure if I should be happy or scarred shitless because either my parents were not at all who I thought they were or aliens had invaded their asses too. I cried and I cried!

Mama came over and joined me on the floor in front of the couch and said, "Thank you, baby. Thank you for finally letting us see our grand child."

"Mama, how did you know?"

"A mama always knows. I knew before you came home those two weeks six years ago. I kept telling your daddy that I kept dreaming about fish but he told me I was just crazy. Then when you came home for those two weeks, I went fishing every night in my dreams and had morning sickness every damn day for the next three months and I knew damn well I wasn't pregnant. So, it had to be you."

"Well, why come you never said anything, Mama?"

She took my hand and said, "Baby, I kept waiting for you to tell me because as much as I talk, it wasn't my truth to tell. But time just kept going by and you never said anything. Then after you left here that day, pretty much stopped calling and hardly ever came home, so I just 'sposed you didn't want us to know, or you was just shame of us. But yo daddy just kept calling me crazy all these years, saying you ain't had no damn grandbaby no where. But I knew, I swear I knew, a mama always knows." She looked over where my daddy and Chelsea were talking nonstop and kept rocking me whispering, "A mama always knows, you hear me Chile, a mama always knows." Then she pulled me by my hand and took me into her bedroom, she pulled out a box from the top of her closet shelf and handed it to me. When I opened the box, there was a baby picture of me, and a picture of me and her from my high school graduation, then underneath that was a calendar from the year Chelsea was born, with dates crossed through but on Nov.15, there was a huge heart circling that date. Lastly, there was a ledger for a savings account for a "Grandbaby Pearson" opened that same year. There was over $15,000 in that account.

Looking at my mama, with pure shock on my face, I think I finally saw her for the very first time. "Mama how did you know that was her birthday and where on earth did you get all this money from?"

She wiped a stray tear; "I felt it all in my bones that day. I'd never hurt like that in my life 'cept for when I was having you. I knew it, I knew you'd had my grand baby on that day. A mama always knows," she said rocking back and forth.

I could not believe my ears, this woman, my mama was amazing, why had I never seen it before, I thought. "Well, what about all this money, where you get that?"

"Chile, I got it from everywhere. From you, from yo daddy, from them heifers whose hair I been doing for years. Hell, I even got it from Farmer's Furniture, cause I stopped running up there getting something new every time I turned around. I had to save it for my grandbaby. I wanted it to have what I couldn't give you so it wouldn't be shame of me like you is." She broke down with sobs. And so did I.

"I'm so sorry, Mama, I'm so sorry...I should have told you Mama, I should have told you." I cried. I cried for all the lost years with my mama, my daddy and my child. I cried and I cried, she rocked and she rocked.

Once I had calmed down, my mama said, "Tell me, now, Chile. Tell me now."

I started from the very beginning and told her everything from the pregnancy, to the adoption, to the reunion. We sat on that bed and bonded more than we'd ever done in life. "Mama, why did you always throw Kevin up in my face then, if you knew?"

"I knew I had never seen you happy other than the time you were with him and I guess I figured if you two could work things out, then everything else would fall into place. I didn't know where my grandbaby was but I figured you two being together was the key to me one day finding out."

"Oh, Mama, I'm so sorry."

"I'm sorry too, Baby. I probably made it hard for you to come to me. I just wanted to push you to be the best and maybe I pushed you away. I was always worried that maybe I wouldn't be around to teach you everything you needed to know in this life that I probably over did it. And when you did not let me in your baby's life, I thought you were ashamed of me, so I just left well enough alone cause I could not take back the past."

"Mama, I'm not ashamed of you, I've never been ashamed of you. You are the toughest woman I know and I admire and envy that about you. I tell everyone, that I may have come from less than humble conditions but I sure as hell didn't come from nothing. I came from a long line of real black women and I'm proud of that! You taught me that, mama, you! I hugged her so tight; I did not want to let go.

I called Jermaine and told him everything, I could hear him sniffling through the phone but he tried to play hard. "Oh, Baby, I'm so happy for you." I asked him if it would be okay if Chelsea and I stayed with my parents tonight and head back in the morning and he said he would miss us but that was the right thing to do.

Chelsea and I enjoyed the rest of the evening with Big Ma, as she affectionately called Mama, and G-Pa, cause my daddy had told her a story about how he used to be an Old G. They loved every minute of it...and so did I.

When they walked us to the car the next morning, they hugged us both so tightly; I thought they would squeeze us to death. I felt awful for putting my parents through this and vowed that from this day forth, I would make it up to them.

HAPPY FATHER'S DAY 30

THIS had been some kind of week, when Chelsea and I got back from my parents' on Tuesday; Jermaine's truck was still in the garage. We both rushed into the house to see him, the den was filled boxes. "Babe," I called out, he came running downstairs and swooped both Chelsea and I up and swung us around. "My girls are home, I missed you both so much!" Then he planted big kisses on both of our faces and we both giggled like schoolgirls.

"What's all this, I asked?" Looking around at all the boxes.

"Well, if you said we are going to be staying here from now on, I figured we would need some cloths. So, since ya'll left me all alone yesterday, I went up and packed up some of our belongings." With a puzzled look on his face, "Are you changing your mind?" He asked nervously.

"Never. I'll never change my mind about this. This has been the best decision I've ever made in my life."

With that, he grabbed my hand, and pulled me behind

him as he ran up the stairs with Chelsea buckling wildly on his back. "Close your eyes Chelsea," he said.

She giggled fiercely. He opened the door to reveal the freshly painted walls with all four of her favorite colors, her white princess bed sat in the middle of the floor and her name was in big, bright white letters on the wall behind the bed. She opened her eyes and screamed in glee. Jumping up and down on her bed, she said, "I love it, I love it, Daddy!"

"I've got one more surprise for you that your Auntie Shayla had custom made especially for you." I just shook my head and smiled, my girl. He went over to the corner where a tablecloth was covering something.

"Can I see, Daddy, please can I see?" Removing the cloth, a 1950's, hand carved, white vanity set, adorned with bright lights, sat eloquently in the corner of Chelsea's room. It was full with jewelry, make-up, shades, headscarves and even boas. Really? Boas? That damn Marilyn, I thought, laughing to myself.

Jermaine said, "Marilyn, I meant Shayla, stopped by yesterday afternoon with it, which is what prompted the full makeover of Chelsea's room." He, Jason, Shayla and Maya had worked all night to get the room finished before we returned. It was just beautiful...as was my life.

That Thursday, I was so nervous as I ran around the house trying to make sure everything was perfect for Jermaine's mother's visit. Lord, please let her like me I thought as I was setting the rest of the table. Chelsea was busy picking up her toys out of the den when she heard the truck doors close, "Mama Joyce!" She jumped up screaming. "Mama Joyce is here, Mama Joyce is here," and she raced me to the door, when I slung the door open; she flew into her grandmother's arms. The silver-haired women, with the smooth mahogany skin hugged Chelsea so tightly, I got lost in the moment. Tears began streaming down my face as I witnessed the pure emotion she felt for my child. Lord, she doesn't have to like me, I thought, as long as she loves my child, that's more than enough. Looking up at me, she whispered, "Thank you," and outstretched her arms to me. This is what unconditional feels like, I thought.

Mama Joyce and I hit it off right away. I loved her French/Creole accent and when she told stories of life in the Bayou, it sounded magical. She told me about some of the antics Jermaine got into as a youth, no surprise there at all. We talked half the night until Jermaine made us wrap it up. He had put Chelsea to bed hours earlier and had retired to our bedroom, while Mama Joyce and I lay across her bed in the guest room and talked about any and everything. I already loved her. Jermaine came to the door around 2am and told his mom he was taking his woman from under her spell. As he reached down and pulled me up, he kissed his mother goodnight and swatted me on the behind and told me to go to bed. Mama Joyce laughed freely. Yes, I really do love her already.

As Jermaine and I cuddled up in our bed, I laid my head on his chest and said, "I love you."

"I love you too," he whispered.

Having Mama Joyce in the kitchen was a big help. She made four pans of peach cobbler, while I made four pans of banana pudding for Maya's Father's Day Extravaganza. What would have taken me four hours; we knocked out in two, now that's teamwork. Jermaine had left at the crack of dawn to go over to help Maya and Jason load up everything they were taking down to his parents', which was practically everything you could imagine. Chelsea woke up this morning like she was doped up on chocolate; she is so excited about going back down to South Georgia to visit Jason's family and I must admit, I am looking forward to seeing everyone as well. I'm also looking forward to introducing everyone to my family this year. Surprisingly, Mama Dearest and my father have agreed to join us for the holiday fun. It's amazing what having grandchildren can do for the soul. My parents have called Chelsea everyday since they met her. They sit on the phone for hours with her talking about absolutely nothing. Unfuckingbelievable, right! Jermaine's been having a field day at my expense, he says I'm hating on my parents. But it's not that, I'm just shocked shitless. We're going to stop through Macon and pick them up on our way down to the Jones' farm, outside of Savannah, once Jermaine gets back with the rental van.

If I'm not mistaken, I think Mama Joyce and Jermaine are just as excited as Chelsea is about seeing the animals. Jermaine teasingly said to his mother, "Mama, according to Jason, animals are not the only thing his hometown has in abundance."

"Really?" Asked Mama Joyce. " What else does small towns have to offer other than country living?"

"Men!" Jermaine and I both said in unison, laughing at the coincidence.

"Ummmmm, interesting." Said Mama Joyce, with a huge grin on her face. "I know you two were trying to be funny but the joke might be on ya'll. Mama needs a good ol' country man!" I laughed so hard until I cried at the look that was now permanent on Jermaine's face.

"Who's hating, now?" I asked.

"Whatever," he said with a scowl.

The drive down was rather pleasant, yet entertaining. My parents fell in love with Mama Joyce and Jermaine right away and vice versa. Mama Joyce and Mama Dearest began exchanging recipes, then home remedies and now they were actually talking about Mama coming out to New Orleans for a visit. I couldn't believe this shit, where the hell is my mama? It was so funny, as we were leaving; all the hens were out on the front stoop. I'm quite sure Mama has been bragging all week, so the rest of those hens had to see it for themselves. She walked down the steps with her chest poked out and her nose in the air; holding onto my daddy's arm like he was Barack Obama and they were marching down the steps of the White House. Lord, I bet those hens haven't stopped cackling yet. But in the words of my mother, "Fuck em!"

The drive from Macon was forty-five minutes, but it

seems like it only took us fifteen because we were having so much fun. We actually talked about perhaps heading on down to Savannah when we left the farm, depending on how tired everyone was. Life is good, I thought, as we pulled off the exit and headed towards the Jones' farm.

I tried to prepare them for what they would see when they got to Jonesville, as Shayla and I affectionately called it. But no one in the car could believe that Jason's family could be as large as I described. "I'm telling ya'll," I said, "Jason has sixteen siblings and each one of the boys have multiplied like their dad, neither with less than four kids; with the exception of Jason, and several have as many as ten. Although most of his sisters were modest in their child birthing, they each have at least two heads of their own. Now, ya'll do the math!" They roared in laughter, still thinking I was playing. "Ya'll gonna see for yourselves! Some shit you just can't make up!" I laughed at the irony of it all, ready to see the look on their faces.

As we turned onto the dirt road that lead to the farm, I swear my parents and Mama Joyce had their heads pressed slam up against the van windows, acting just like little kids that had never been anywhere. As the grand, Tudor farmhouse came into view, they really started oooohhing and ahhhhhing, even worse than Chelsea. "Look, Mommy, look," said Chelsea pointing at the giant water slide and jumping house adorning the front lawn.

"Oh, Lord, Jesus, look over there, they got a dunking booth, a cotton candy machine, they're popping popcorn and making funnel cakes...this ain't no bar-b-que, this a got damn fair." We all fell out laughing as Mama tried to cover her mouth, remembering Chelsea was in the car.

Chelsea leaned over, kissed her on the cheeks and said, "It's okay, Big Ma, cause I was thinking the same thing!" We all laughed but if I'm not mistaken, my mama was back there giggling.... just like she did in that principal's office that day so long ago. Well, I be damn, I thought. I can't wait to tell Shayla about this shit.

"What is that area they have all roped off over there?" Jermaine asked.

Pointing out everything for them, I said, "That is actually where we will be playing relay games later on, which is why Mr. Jones have the lines chalked off like that."

"Can I play, too?" Chelsea asked excitedly.

"Yes, dear, you absolutely may. They have designed the games so the adults and kids can play together and create lasting memories for generations to come. They also have old school contest, like double dutch and hoola hoop that the kids and adults can compete in; as well as, and," I said excitedly, "at the end of the night they have a giant soul train line followed by the most beautiful fireworks you ever could see. When I said, Jason's family is the bomb, I meant it!" Everyone laughed ferociously.

Before Jermaine could park the car, Chelsea spotted Maya and Shayla, and out the door she went, right into their outstretched arms. "TeTe Maya, Auntie Shayla," she yelled as she dashed across the yards. Both were ecstatic, understandably so, because she really was all of our baby. They'd gone through the storm and weathered it right along beside me. And then when I had to make the ultimate sacrifice and give her up, they had to be strong enough for me too. If it were not for those two, I would have never gotten out of that dark place that my mind drifted to right after giving birth to Chelsea. While, Shayla stayed pissed for a little while because she was the last one to find out about the adoption, she never left my side. I tried to explain to her that I didn't tell Maya either but she'd figured it out when she saw me and Mr. D., talking with a strange, white lady inside the apartment one day when she came home from work early. It wasn't that I was trying to be selfish or leave them out of the decision making process, I just knew how much the decision was going to hurt them and I was just simply trying to prolong them the pain that I was already feeling. When you love someone, the last thing on earth you want to do is hurt them.

Shaking my head to snap out of that place inside my head marked "FRAGILE," I began making introductions; although, by now Maya had provided her in-laws with a brief synopsis of my situation so all the introductions went smoothly. Everyone offered their sincerest congratulations and told me how much I deserved happiness...and for once in my life, I was inclined to believe that.

The evening was going fantastic. My family was enjoying all the festivities laid out by the Jones clan.

Chelsea was a no call, no show. She was having so much fun running and playing with the hundreds of grandkids, she forgot our asses even existed. If we didn't call for her, she wasn't showing her face! Mama Joyce was in hog heaven! I looked up one time and she was actually out in the garden with Ma Dukes, picking some kind of damn vegetables. Really? Where the hell they do that at?

Jermaine, of course, had hit it off right away with all of Jason's brothers and Mr. Jones, the patriarch of the family. Surprisingly, Ma Dukes said he was the "finest, chocoltiest thing she'd ever seen and he shole ran circles around pretty ass Steven." Poor Steven, he'd only met them once but they never took a liking to him. Ma Dukes always said he had shifty eyes and you could not trust a Negro with shifty eyes. But Jermaine, on the other hand, had jumped right on in, talking trash and holding his own, which is the only way to survive with this bunch. I glanced over at him at the spades table talking cash money shit, and in that instant my heart smiled.

Of course, my mama was a crowd hit, with all that mouth of hers. At one point, her and Shayla had tagged team one of Jason's brothers up in a corner and had him speechless. Mama actually told him that Shayla D. had got inducted into her "big girl panties" from her and her crew and she knew damn well she could handle anything he had to offer. Then she touched him on his muscular chest and said, "But what she can't handle, a bitch like me will!" Everyone was on their knees laughing, especially Jason's dad, whom I think took great pride in his sons' reputations with the ladies.

I went over whining to my dad, who was sitting over at picnic table feeding one of the twins some watermelon, "Daaaaa-dddie, please make her stop, pleasssssse."

"Baby, let her be. She's all mouth, she won't bust a grape in a fruit fight." Everyone laughed. "I learnt a long time ago to pick my battles where yo mama is concerned and her and that fast ass mouth ain't a battle worth fighting...cause I'd loose."

Jermaine walked up and put his arms around my waist and teasingly said, "I guess I better take G-Pa's advice on that too, because the apple didn't fall far from the tree." Pouting, I pushed him off of me.

Just then, a loud commotion came from the front side of the house. All we could hear were hundreds of loud screams. "Oh my God!" one of the adults yelled as we all jumped up and raced around to the front side of the house, praying none of the kids were seriously hurt. That seemed like the longest distance I've ever had to travel; as I'm sure it felt that way for every adult that had kids out there. Of course, most of the men made it around front faster, and then the screams got even louder and all I could do was just stop because the pit in the center of my stomach told me something was terribly wrong. "Lord, please let my baby be okay!" I said aloud as I rounded the corner.

Once I had a vision of the throng that had formed, I could tell that the screams were not of terror but of delight. Everyone; men, women and children, were jumping up and down, screaming hysterically. They were crowded around some guy standing next to a Black Stretched Hummer Limo...then I felt it. The magnet.

Kevin turned and looked dead at me. My heart stopped.

I cannot remember what happened next or how I got to the back bedroom, all I could remember was opening my eyes and seeing Maya, Shayla, my parents and Mr. D, all starring down at me. "What the hell is he doing here?" Maya asked, with venom spilling from her veins like she was revisiting that dreadful day in our past. Everyone turned to look at Mama Dearest.

"I don't know what the hell ya'll looking at me for, I didn't do it!" Mama huffed.

Just then the door opened, Jermaine and Jason strolled in merrily, "What the hell ya'll doing back here with all the excitement going on outside?" Jason asked.

"Yeah, Babe!" Jermaine stretched his hands to me, "I want you meet my boy, I know you don't like football and all but I promise, you're going to love my boy Kevin." If only you knew, I thought to myself.

"Hold on, Jermaine," Mama muttered, but for once her mouth wasn't loud enough.

Jermaine had pulled me to my feet and was leading me out the door. "It can wait, Big Ma," he yelled back over his shoulder. "Come on, I want you all to meet my boy, Kev. He won't be able to stay long." As Jermaine pulled me up the hallway, I vaguely heard Jason excitedly calling out the stats of the great Kevin Williams, Heisman Trophy Winner, Pro Bowl Wide Receiver for the Philadelphia Eagles, two times Super Bowl MVP...please GOD help me.

As we approached the door, I could see through the cloud of haze covering my face, Mama Joyce and Kevin sharing a warm embrace, as he chowed down on the amazing bar-b-que ribs, specialty of Jason's uncle. When the door opened, Kevin looked in our direction and stood nervously "Why me, God, I thought?" Jermaine's words came out of nowhere because in my head I was having a mild stroke. "Kev, this is the lovely lady I was telling you about, the lady that has made all my dreams come true. The mother of my child and if she would have me, my future wife, Nicolette Pearson."

The world seemed to cease on its axis at this very moment, with unmistaken hatred in his eyes, Kevin extended his hand, "Nice to meet you, Ni-co-lette." He sounded my name out like he was taking speech therapy and it was the first time he'd ever uttered the word.

My hand was shaking and sweating feverishly but somehow I managed to reciprocate his handshake. "Nice to meet you." I stammered with a lowered head. In his excitement, Jermaine didn't even notice my or my family's trepidation. He proceeded in making introductions of the rest of the gang. Then a wave of silence hovered over the crowd like the plague. I just knew Jermaine would be able to hear my heart beating erratically inside my chest. As if on queue, Shayla swooped in to save the day, full Marilyn mode. "Kevin Williams, The Kevin Williams," she drooled in the sultriest voice I've ever heard her muster. Strolling slowly and sexily over to him, she walked right up to him and putting her hands on his chest before continuing, making sure she had everyone's undivided attention. Jermaine and Jason were on their knees laughing at Shayla's usual antics and at the shocked expression daunting Kevin's face. "I have been waiting a lifetime to see you and the things I've always wanted to say to you are too much for these mere mortals." Pouting up her ruby reds lips sexily, in pure Marilyn fashion. She turned to us and winked sexily as she nestled close to Kevin and pulled him away from the group. My girl. Everyone laughed, and then Maya told me and Mama to come help her in the kitchen, while the men went back to ogling the NFL great and discussing his pending trade.

I sat at the kitchen table in a trance. Mama was pacing around the room talking to herself and Maya was leaning over the stove saying a silent prayer. We sat there like this, each deep in thought, for about twenty more minutes. Then we heard the screen door creep open and in strolled Marilyn, I meant, Shayla, my girl. As she slung herself in the seat next to me, all acting out the window, she said, "We got a problem, a big problem!" Tears sprang to her eyes, real ones. "He says he wants custody of his daughter," she said point blank and then started to cry.

Before I became hysterical, Mama Dearest grabbed me and Maya grabbed Shayla and led us through the house to the back bedroom, out of sight and out of ear shout of any on listeners. My mama sat me on the edge of the bed and rocked me as I cried uncontrollably. Maya said, "Okay, Shayla tell us exactly what he said."

"Well," Shayla sniffled. "He said Nikki ain't shit and she did not deserve to raise Chelsea after she had given her up for adoption and kept him from knowing he even had a child. He said; even though Jermaine is his boy and he don't want to see him hurt, he was not going to stand aside while his daughter call some other nigga daddy and if we thought so, we got another thing coming."

"How did he find out?" Asked Mama.

"Yeah, he's pissed off about that too," said Shayla. "He said just imagine how his mama felt when she found out she had a grandchild on Facebook! He said, Mrs. Pam called him all hysterical talking about somebody called her and said Nikki had came home to see her parents with a little girl talking about that was her daughter. So, she went on my face book page, from someone else's page, cause she ain't my friend, and saw pictures of us all from that first day we met Chelsea. She then called him and told him about it and told him to look for his self. She said although Chelsea looks just like Nikki's high yella ass, she did have some of his features and she knew that was her grandbaby. He thought she was just talking though, so he didn't pay her any attention at first but she kept on, so he finally went and checked it out and imagine his surprise when he saw Nikki, his boy, Jermaine, and his little girl all playing in the pool like one big, happy family."

"So he said he called Jermaine and chatted with him to

catch up and sure enough, unbeknownst to Jermaine, he filled the asshole in on all the details of what had been going on in his life recently."

"How do they even know each other, Jermaine don't play no damn football?" Maya asked.

"He said he met Jermaine after Hurricane Katrina, he and some of his teammates flew down to New Orleans to help with disaster relief. His foundation contracted Jermaine's construction company to build homes for fifty families who had lost everything in the flood. He said, he and Jermaine hit it off right away, and have been cool every since. He said, although, his hectic schedule don't allow him time to visit much, they talk on the phone often."

"Well, I be damn!" Mama summed it up for all of us.

NOT THIS TIME 31

"UNFUCKINGBELIEVABLE!" I said aloud. Obviously scarring the shit out of the other three in the room because they looked at me like I'd lost my mind. I guess they thought I was going to be catatonic forever. Oh, hell, nawl, not if that bastard thought he was going to take my baby from me. Standing up, with strength I didn't know I had, I said, "That bastard has lost his fucking mind if he think he's gonna come up in here and take my baby! Oh, hell nawl!" Just as me and my posse headed towards the door, it opened, Ma Dukes was standing there with that, "Oh, hell nawl" look on her face too.

Ma Dukes looked me directly in the eye and said in no uncertain terms, "Start talking!"

We all sat down and I recounted the events of my life

to the elder that I've grown to love and respect so much. When I was done, I asked, "How did you know something was wrong?"

Shaking her head, Ma Dukes said quietly, "A mama knows." We all nodded our heads in understanding.

Standing, speaking up loud and clearly pissed, I said, "That man has took enough from me, I'm not letting him take my child and my man away from me too!"

All the ladies looked around shocked. Then burst out laughing and began high-fiving one another. "That's my girl!" I heard mama say, with pure pride in her voice.

As I headed toward the door for the second time, Ma Dukes stopped me and said, "Hold up, Chile." Taking me by my shoulders and looking me squarely in the eyes. "There's a time and a place for everything, this ain't the time nor the place. What you gonna do is go out there and enjoy the rest of the day with that fine, chocolate man that nice woman out there done birthed." Everyone laughed, all having grown fond of Mama Joyce. "Then ya'll gonna get in that van, drop Joyce and Chelsea off with your parents in Macon for a few days, then head home and make love to that man like your life depends on it. Then and only then, are you going to tell him the absolute truth about that piece of shit and together you two are going to decide what's best for ya'll family. You hear what I'm saying?" Speechless, all I could do was nod my head in agreement.

"Dammnnn!" Mama, Maya and Shayla screamed at the

same time. "Ma Dukes, you got a little freak in you I see!" Said Shayla. We all laughed

"How in the hell you thank I got all them damn chillum?" She asked, laughing at herself. Then she said seriously, "Oh and as for Mr. Heisman Trophy, his ass should be gone by now!"

We all looked around at each other bewildered, then she said, "Yeah, as soon as I saw something wasn't right, I started putting two and two together. So, I fixed his ass a big plate and a to-go box, cause we believe in feeding folk 'round here, then I called him over to a seat and whispered in his ear, "I don't know what you up to but it ain't happening here. You eat this here food; you talk to 'dese here men folk for a hot minute and you sign some autographs for dem' chillum and then you take that to-go box and get the hell off my property with that bullshit, cause this ain't what you want!" I think it must've scared the shit out of him when he looked around at them big ass boys of mine. But what he don't know is them boys of mine ain't gonna do nothing but laugh, tell lies and make babies...it's dem' mean ass girls of mine he had to worry about! We all laughed uncontrollably, as she hugged me in a warm embrace and we all walked back outside. Kevin was nowhere in sight.

We enjoyed the rest of the evening and as the fireworks erupted in the night sky, I knew I wasn't going to allow anyone to steal my joy, no, not this time.

The two and a half hour drive back to Alpharetta was the

longest ride of my life. Everyone else in the van, including Mama Dearest, seemed to be having the time of their lives. Chelsea really had a knack with Jermaine and her grandparents because they all clearly adored her. She was still bouncing off the wall from her day in the country and was reliving every minute of it as she gave us all the full run down, just like we were not there too. When she held up her coloring book and said, "Mama look, I got a autograph," I felt like all the blood had somehow leaked right out of my body. Glancing down at Kevin's signature, all I could do was shake my head.

After dropping my parents, Mama Joyce and Chelsea off at my parents' home in Macon, I faked a headache and pretended to sleep all the way home. Every so often, I peeped out of the corner of my eyes at Jermaine's handsome profile. This man, my man, did not deserve this. Having gone through so much just because he loved MY child, how can I add any more heartache to him? Closing my eyes, I wondered, what did I ever do to God to make him hate me so much? I tried to be a good child when I was coming up, never gave Mama Dearest any problems, partly because I was more scarred of her ass than God himself. After I had Chelsea, I finished college, got a good job, went to church, paid my tithes and sent money home to my mama. So why did God hate me? Trying to fight back tears, I really did fall into a restless sleep.

When I awoke, the house was quiet and Jermaine's side was empty, I leapt up from my covers screaming his name, "Noooooooo, I cried, it wasn't a dream, he left me for real! Frantically, I looked around the room, and then I spotted a note on the nightstand. Reading the note, I sighed and pressed it close to my heart, his cologne massaging my nostrils. Work, he's gone to work. I've never felt so happy and so sad at the same damn time! My man was just gone to work!

As I lay in bed, all I could think about was Kevin's no good ass having the audacity to stroll in like he was father of the fucking year talking about taking my baby...nigga please. I opened my purse and pulled out the card, Shayla had discreetly placed inside yesterday. As I starred at the card, which adorned a half naked picture of Kevin holding his helmet, I thought.... this is just like the conceited bastard to have a business card with his fucking body on it...where the hell they do that at? Reaching for my cell, I angrily dialed the number. When I heard the baritone of his voice say "Hello", I lost all of my cool. My mind went back to how the bastard had cheated on me with anybody that had a coochie, and how scarred I was walking around Spelman's campus not knowing how I was going to raise a baby alone. Then my mind drifted inside that cold, dark delivery room and how I felt my life would end when I heard my baby's cry, then saw a caseworker whisk her out of the delivery room before I could even lay an eye on her.

"You selfish bastard" I yelled into the receiver. "If you think you're going to come in here and take my baby then you got another thing coming to you!" I could hear him stammering trying to get something out but at this very moment, I was Mama Dearest's daughter in every way because I wouldn't let the bastard get a word in. "If you wanted a baby so fucking bad, then maybe you shouldn't have paid that white bitch off to have an abortion and I'm sure there were plenty more after that. You ain't shit, you ain't never been shit and you ain't never gonna be shit! You don't give a damn about Chelsea; the only person you give a fuck about is you. So fuck you and fuck your nosey ass mama and tell her to stay the fuck out of my business!" Slamming the phone down, I have never felt so liberated in my life. Before, I could start to feel sorry for myself, I jumped up, threw on some cloths and headed straight for Mr. D's law firm. My cell was ringing non-stop. Fuck Kevin and the horse he rode in on.

OH, HELL NAWL 32

AS I walked through my front door, I noticed the house
was dimly lit and had lit candles carefully placed
throughout the downstairs. I could hear the late, Gerald
Levert's sultry voice belting out one of my all-time
favorites, "*Baby, Hold on to me...see I'm a special kind. A
good man is hard to find, told you a thousand times...Baby,
Hold on to Me*" blasting from the interior speakers. After
the music had quickly got me in the mood, my nostrils
were then assaulted by the tantalizing aroma of steak and
lobster coming from the kitchen. Instead of feeling like
the happiest woman on earth as I did just a week ago, by
the time Jermaine rounded the corner with a glass of
wine, I felt like I was about to crumble up and die right
there in the middle of my living room floor. My man really
was too damn good for me. Damn Kevin's stupid ass!

As he handed me the glass of wine he was holding, he
pulled me into a warm embrace, dipping his head, his
tongue encircled mine in a tantalizing waltz inside my
mouth. Momentarily, I was lost in this man. I'd forgotten
about Kevin's conceited ass, I'd forgotten what Mr. D. and

his associates said about Kevin still having parental rights because he'd never consented to an adoption, I'd forgotten what they said about me not having any rights to Chelsea at all...all I could think about was this man, my man, that I loved so much; this very man, the only man on earth who I'd lay down my life for. Just as our kiss was about to head in another direction, the doorbell rang. Pulling back, I looked from Jermaine to the door, puzzled. Lightly chuckling, he strolled over to the door, "Don't worry, Honey, it's just Shayla." Shayla? I was so confused, what is she doing here?

When Jermaine opened the door, Shayla strolled into the room in full Marylyn mode, doing a fancy twirl to show off her latest ensemble. Laughing uncontrollably, "Oh, so I guess you're gone with the wind fabulous today, huh?"

Air kissing both of Jermaine's cheeks, "Not just today, EVERYDAY" she drooled. We were literally killing ourselves laughing at this fool, if nothing else, she was always good for a dramatic entrance and even more dramatic exit and a lot of laughs in between. My girl.

As if on queue, Shayla glanced around the dimly lit room and said, "What the hell is this?" I don't know what kind of freaky shit ya'll into but it ain't that type of party!"

Laughing uncontrollably, cause this time she wasn't acting at all, she was totally serious and looked to be having a mild heart attack. Jermaine spoke up and said, "Don't worry Shayla, we don't get down like that either. I have a surprise for you..." Just as he was about to finish his sentence, the doorbell rang again. Shayla and I both were completely lost, but just as Jermaine strolled back over to the door, I think Shayla and I were both figuring it out at the same damn time. "What up, Kev; come on in." My heart stopped and the glass of wine slipped right out of my hand. The clattering of the glass shattering on the floor brought all the pleasantries to a halt. Even, Shayla, I mean Marylyn, couldn't respond fast enough to divert the attention off of me this time "Oh, Sweetheart, I'm sorry." Jermaine, said to me. "I know it's not everyday that a big time celebrity comes to dinner and your place, I guess I should have told you but I didn't want you to spoil the surprise for Shayla."

With a devious chuckle, Kevin's eyes never left mine, while Shayla and I just starred eerily at one another for a brief moment. Recovering quickly, Shayla sprang into pure Marylyn mode as she strolled over to Kevin, placing a sexy peck on his cheek and said, "Why Mr. Williams, what do I owe such a wonderful surprise?" Wrapping her arms into his, she pulled him down to the den, engaging in small talk, until they were out of earshot of Jermaine and myself.

Taking a page out of Shayla's, I meant Marylyn's handbook, I said, "Honey, why don't you go fix our guest a glass of wine and another one for me, while I get this mess cleaned up."

Kissing me lightly on the cheek, he said, "No problem, Baby. I'm glad you aren't mad for me springing this on you at the last minute but my boy, Kevin, had really taken a liking to Shayla yesterday."

"Oh, Baby, I appreciate you looking out for my girl. "As he turned to walk away, I reached out and pinched him on his sexy butt, he giggled just like a schoolgirl. Damn, I love that man.

Trying to stop my hands from shaking, I contemplated on the best way to handle the situation. Lord, six months ago, when Steven's selfish ass was laying up in here sponging off of me, would I ever had imagined my life to have changed so drastically in such a short period of time. Feeling helpless for only the second time in my life, I remembered how my mama would always say, "As stinky as it is…shit happens! You just better be ready to clean it up!" And that's just what I'm going to do!

I tried to remain as calm as possible throughout the course of dinner. It was damn near sickening to watch Kevin fawning all over Shayla and Marylyn or not, this bitch seemed to really be enjoying the attention. As I chewed on a piece of the succulent lobster tail Jermaine had prepared, I watched as she instinctively responded to his hand on her bare back, did I just see lust flash across this bitch face? "Ok, Nikki, get yourself together, you're just hallucinating!" I said to myself, but at that very moment, something deep in my soul told me that a storm was brewing and it wasn't going to be pretty. Throughout dinner, I could feel Kevin's eyes on me, almost assaulting me with his penetrating accusatory gaze. Oblivious to Jermaine, every time Kevin mentioned Chelsea's name, I was raging inside while I put on a perfect production of Martha Stewart meets June Clever, totally Shayla, I meant Marylyn worthy.

Finally, Shayla, after catching my questioning gazes at some of her involuntary responses to Kevin, announced that she had a long day tomorrow and needed to get on home. Before I could offer to walk her outside, Kevin jumped his happy ass up and offered to walk her outside. I could have stabbed them both right there , dead in their hearts. Instead, I grabbed Jermaine's hand as we walked them to the door. As Shayla turned to thank us for dinner, she couldn't even look me in my eyes; instead she began performing in full Marylyn mode, even bowing talking about, "Sir Jermaine and Me'Lady in her full England accent, thoust have a wonderful night," and sauntered off like her chariot was awaiting. While Jermaine and Kevin thought that shit was just fucking hilarious, my blood was boiling inside, because I knew that shit was her defense mechanism. This bitch was feeling Kevin. My girl?

While helping Jermaine clean up the kitchen, my mind was racing a mile a minute. I was trying desperately to be nonchalant as he went on and on about how it was time for Kevin to settle down and start a family of his own and how it may take someone like him to tame Shayla's wild ass down. I was thinking, "Oh imma tame her ass alright." Then he interrupted my thoughts, "Babe, what do you think about Kevin?"

"He seems nice enough, I guess. I'm just not so sure he's right for Shayla though," I said honestly.

"Really, why not?" "I thought they complemented each other rather nicely."

Cause he used to complement me rather nicely, I thought. Thinking it was safer to change the subject I said, " I don't know, maybe you're right. What time are you going to pick up Chelsea and Mama Joyce tomorrow?"

"Actually, I spoke to your pops this afternoon and he said him and your mom was going to bring them back this weekend. I guess he noticed the look of disbelief that crossed my face. "Yeah, he said they never came to see your new home and better late than never." Well, I be damn, is all I could think. It was amazing how one little girl could be added to an equation that had been fucked up and completely unsalvageable for years, and immediately set everything on its axis. Sending everything and everybody who loved her into a harmonious orbit. I loved that little girl with all my heart.

All that talk about my parents suddenly made my mind drift back to when I was just a little older than Chelsea is now, sitting Indian style in that tiny bedroom of that dilapidated project smelling like collard greens, ox tails and burnt hair. Notice I said "that" bedroom because Mama Dearest always made it clear in no uncertain terms that I didn't own a damn thing around there, cause my name wasn't on shit. I wanted to tell her so many times, you don't own shit either, cause your name might be on something but it was a rental agreement and not a damn mortgage, so we were both borders. But of course, I never got the balls to say half the shit I really wanted to say. On that particular day though, I sat in the middle of my bed crying, holding that black ass doll with that nappy ass hair, every little black girl in the world had, cause it was the only black doll they made at the time. Mama was screaming at the top of her lungs that she was gonna fuck my daddy up and that, no-good, back stabbing whore of his and all my daddy kept saying was, "You so fucking crazy, you're the reason why I went over there!" Then I heard my mama say, "Oh, Imma show you crazy and when I'm done, imma send your ass back over there; and then she started chasing after him with the big ole' butcher knife she had been cutting up collard greens with. My daddy, or that man, cause that's all I called him back then, ran into my mama's bedroom and locked the door. As I ran into the hallway, begging mama to stop, all I could see was my mama stabbing that door trying to cut her way into the room trying to get him. The next thing I knew, the cops were dragging my mama out the apartment, she still had the knife in her hands and was screaming at my daddy, "Imma kill you, you low down dirty bastard and you tell my so-called friend, whenever and wherever I see her ass, that's where they gonna be picking up her body from." As the cops pulled away with Mama Dearest banging hysterically on the back window, that man put his hand on my shoulder and said, "Stop crying, everything gone be alright." I remember snatching my body away from him, I walked back in the house, picked up the phone and called Shayla and she said don't worry, my daddy will go get her. Shayla, my girl.

As Jermaine got in the hot shower, I pretended to be looking for some new shower gel I wanted to try, while in actuality I sent two texts. The first one was to Maya, it said: You ain't gonna believe this shit! The last one was to Shayla, it said: Really, Bitch? Really?

Just as I expected, Maya had been blowing my cell up all night, even though I'd texted her back and told her I was turning the ringer off. She was so inpatient, she was just as predictable as stripper at a Super Bowl party. As soon as Jermaine left for work, I called her back and filled her in on all the details from the night before.

Being the voice of reason she said, "Nikki, are you sure you're not making this connection up between Kevin and Shayla? For as long as I've known you, Shayla has always had your back if no one else's. I know she loves you more than anything. I don't see her ever hurting you like that."

"I know she loves me but I know damn well I didn't make up what I saw in her eyes last night. It was as if she had a reaction to him that even she couldn't control and Marylyn my ass, that bitch was not pretending. If anything, she was trying to pretend like what was happening wasn't really happening. Not to mention, I ain't heard shit from that ho since she sashayed out my fucking door. Since when have you known that bitch not to have something to say?"

"Damnnnnnnnn," was all Maya could muster through the phone.

"My mama always said, "Never let your friends know what your man is working with, cause when good dick is involved, friendship goes straight out the window...right along with their stank-ass drawers." Shaking my head, I got even more pissed thinking about where those two went and what they did last night after leaving my house.

"I just can't believe Shayla would do what you're suggesting. I'm about to call her on the three-way right now. Hold on. " As I waited anxiously for Shayla to answer her line, my mind drifted back to all the things we'd been through together and I would never have believed she would hurt me. Just as Maya was about to hang up, Shayla answered the phone in the smallest voice I've ever heard come from her throat. I guess that shit threw Maya's ass off too because she began stuttering, "Ar-r-are you okay?" Asked Maya.

"Yeah, girl," she said shyly. "I'm okay, I just can't talk right now."

It was literally killing me inside to hold the receiver and not say anything, which was not my intention when Maya initially called but after hearing Shayla's discombobulated voice, I was stuck. Then, I honestly felt like everything inside me had died when Maya asked her, "Do you have company?" And she said yes and hung up the fucking phone! Oh, Hell Nawl!

MR. TOO DAMN GOOD 33

AS the days turned to weeks, my life seemed to be in a
tailspin. While trying to play merry homemaker to
Jermaine and Mother of the Year to Chelsea, inside I felt
like I was about to lose my fucking mind. Although, I had
not heard anything else from Kevin about custody of
Chelsea, neither had I heard from my best friend in the
world! It seemed like every other day though, Kevin was
either texting Jermaine or they were meeting to "just
hang out." Just hang out my ass, that bastard was up to
something, I could feel it in my bones, like my mama used
to say. Speaking of my mama, I never realized just how
insightful she was. With all that's going on in my life, she
and I had have become closer than we ever have. And
now, instead of calling Maya or Shayla's trifling ass, I turn
to my mama. I never in a million years would have
imagined that we would talk damn near every day but
sure enough if a day has gone by and she hasn't called me,
I was calling her. I will admit, it honestly feels great to

finally have a bond with my mother that went beyond DNA. I actually love talking to her and now I realize what Shayla (with her trifling ass) had been telling me for years. My mama is real as fuck...she says whatever the fuck she wants and means that shit too and whosoever don't like it can kiss her ass!

A smile crept across my face just as I thought about what Mama Dearest said yesterday afternoon when I was having yet another one of my mini breakdowns after I saw Jermaine watching an interview of Kevin on ESPN talking about his recent trade and how happy he was to be back in the A, playing for his home team. He was standing inside the Falcons' locker room with nothing on but some red gym shorts, with sweat drenching down his chest like he had just finished a work out. All I could imagine was Shayla's trifling ass riding that big, black dick of his and I literally got sick to my stomach. Not wanting to alarm Jermaine, I dashed up the stairs and by the time I made it to the bathroom, I was vomiting everywhere. All I could do was sit on the cold, tiled floor with my back against the door, and cry my eyes out. I sounded like a wounded animal as I wept into the thick towel I was using to muffle the sound. After about twenty minutes, I turned the water on in my deep; claw foot tub so Jermaine could not hear me, then called my mama and cried some more.

After my mama had tried to console me for about thirty minutes, she finally gave up and said, "Listen Baby, I'm going to say this as politely as I can 'cause I know your heart aching right now, but If you don't stop all this damn crying and stop feeling sorry for yourself, I know something! Now, I didn't raise no Punk Bitch and it's high time for you to stop acting like one. First of all, call Mr. D., with his fine ass, and tell him the real reason you have been ignoring his calls. You tell him, his daughter ain't shit! Hell, he know better than anybody that he raised a ho! Hell, her mama was a ho, she ain't stole a damn thing! You tell him all about her fucking Kevin and how you didn't want to put him in the middle of ya'll mess. But, I'll tell you this...right or wrong that man loves his daughter but he loves you too. Let him help you!"

IRRELEVANT 34

"HONEY I invited Kevin over for dinner, I hope you don't mind," Jermaine yelled from inside our bedroom.

Looking up into the bathroom mirror where I was standing brushing my teeth, I'd never been so thankful to have a mouthful of Listerine in my entire life because my first instinct was to scream out, "He'll yeah I mind!" I don't want that lowlife bastard anywhere near me or my daughter and I sure as hell don't want him sitting at my dinner table!" But instead, I nodded my head in agreement.

Damn, I love this man! I don't know what I would do if I lose him or Chelsea for that matter. It has been three weeks since I'd spoke with Mr.D. and he told me to tell Jermaine everything so we can get him on board but every time I try to broach the subject, I literally get sick to my stomach. Just the other night, we had finished making passionate love and just as he often did, he pulled me close, kissed me tenderly on the lips then rolled me over and began massaging me slowly and thoroughly all over.

He knew how much I loved when his big, strong but tender hands played a symphony over my body, relaxing me, often sending me into a deep sleep. However, instead of making me drift off to Never-never land like it usually did, it made me want to open up and make everything right between us. Keeping secrets from the man that had grown to mean so much to me was driving me crazy. But as soon as I got ready to open my mouth, I could feel an explosion of vile open up in my esophagus and spill right up through the crevices of my throat and before I knew it, I was vomiting everywhere! Jermaine jumped up with worry lines etched all over his face, ran to the restroom and grabbed the garbage can. Running back, he held the garbage can up to my mouth and rubbed my tousled sandy hair back away from my face, uttering words of comfort and love. Once I was done, he ran a tub of hot water, lovingly lifted me from the soiled bed and sat me in the deep claw foot tub, where he gently bathed me and washed my hair. If I wasn't so sick to my stomach, I would have gave him the best blow job he had ever had in his life because that act of kindness was the sweetest thing any man has ever did for me. I knew then and there, that there was nothing and no one I would let come between us. I loved this man with all my heart and I planned on spending the rest of my life showing him the depth of my love.

Just as I was putting the finishing touch on the loose chignon I had placed strategically on top of my head, my cell phone rang. Jermaine stopped putting the pillows on the bed and looked dead into the mirror at my shocked expression. Damn, why didn't I take that stupid ass ringtone off my phone like I'd meant to. He watched as I walked gingerly over to the bedside table where my phone was lying, the sound of Jagged Edge still escaping the speaker of the phone..." *I gotta be the one you love, I gotta be the one you touch, I gotta be the one to fill your life with sunshine...*" Pressing ignore on the phone, I looked at Jermaine as he turned to leave and saw the hurt in his eyes and all I could think is... " I gotta be alright...I gotta be the biggest dummy on the planet!" Running down stairs after Jermaine was pointless, by the time I got to the landing, I could hear the roar of his engine. And to make matters worse, Chelsea ran up the stairs straight for me and said, "What did you do to my Daddy?"

Tears sprang to my eyes as I tried to reassure my daughter that Daddy was just in a hurry, that he was fine. But Chelsea, the little spawn of mother dearest, was not falling for it. She looked me dead in the eyes and said matter of factly, "He better be alright!" Then just like that, she turned and ran back down to her fort in front of the giant Plasma, where Hannah Montana was just going on stage to perform for her friends.

"Look at this shit," I said to myself. I got baby mama drama, my man don't trust me, I just got checked by my six year old and that little skank, MIley Cyrus, is getting more love in my house than I am! Ain't that a bitch!

Heading back in my bedroom, I could hear the sound of Jagged Edge again blasting from my cell. Snatching the phone up, I yelled," What do you want?"

Steven's voice came back over the airwaves barely above a whisper, " I want you."

I could not believe my ears, the audacity of this fool to call me up like I was his revolving door and was just sitting around waiting on his ass to realize he fucked up. " Nigga, please! You had your chance, you didn't appreciate me then so to hell with you now!"

Just as I was about to slam the phone shut, I heard him say, "Nikki, hold up, please just hear me out!" Sighing heavily into the phone, I held the phone intently as he began to sob. "Nikki, I know I messed up... I didn't treat you the way you deserved to be treated. I'm s-o-rr-ry," he sobbed in my ear. As Steven continued on and on about how he should've put me first and how his life hasn't been the same the past few months without me, my mind drifted back to another time. When Steven and I first met, our lives could not have been better. What began as a wonderful friendship blossomed into a glorious and fulfilling relationship. There was nothing we could not talk about, often finishing each other's thoughts. There was never a dull moment when we were together.

When we decided to move in together I was on top of the world. Our tiny, dank apartment over in West End felt like it was a mansion in the center of Paris, as long as we were together. We spent countless nights eating Raman noodles and challenging each other to games of Wheel of Fortune and Jeopardy. I never would have guessed our lives would have spiraled so far away from one another in such a short period of time. But once, I got my position at

Globalnomics, our relationship gradually started to change.

Steven often accused me of " thinking you all that now!" What the hell did that mean? Just because I had to buy a new wardrobe for my job, I guess that made me "all that". It wasn't like I could just stroll my black ass up in Globalnomics, an international marketing firm, wearing the same acid washed jeans and tight tank top that I'd worn to catch the bus heading to Spelman everyday. It was like he resented me for following my dreams. But when he met me I was in grad school... what the hell did he think I was going to do with the damn degree... roll that bitch up and smoke it?

I tried my best to please him as I held onto this unrealistic ideal of what our lives were supposed to be. But the harder I fought to make things better, the more he pulled away from me. I'll never forget the day I closed on this house... I was sure it was the beginning of something beautiful. I couldn't have been further from the truth. When we left out of the attorney's office, I felt like I was walking on sunshine like Cindy Lauper in the 80's. The first thing I wanted to do was call my girls on my way to christening my new home with the love of my life. The closer we got to my new Alpharetta subdivision, the worse his mood got. When we finally got to the front door, I waited for him to pick me up and carry me across the threshold. But nooooo, Mr. Wonderful kicked my fucking door off the hinges and turned around and began yelling at me talking about how I made him look like a fool in front of them white folks. I was appalled, crying hysterically, I begged him to calm down and to tell me what I did wrong. As he hurled his keys at the wall he said that I just sat there with this goofy as grin on my face and let them white folks treat him like he wasn't shit. He went on this long tirade about how he ain't my bitch and how I ain't going to be treating him like he's my bitch. He said, if I were a good woman I never would have let them crackers act like he was irrelevant. As if my next breath was dependent on it, I grabbed him around his ankles from where I was kneeled down on the plush carpet crying and begged him to forgive me. He looked down at me with a cold, hard stare that I'd never seen before, then hurled spit in my face and walked out the house and sped away... in my car.

Now, as I sit on the phone listening to him beg me to take him back, I can't believe I was so gullible and naive. Hell yeah, he was irrelevant to those crackers, as he would say. It wasn't like they needed his signature on anything. Hell, his credit was so jacked up, the credit bureau just stopped issuing him a FICA score, they said they had better stuff to do with their time. He was a non-fucking factor then and he's a non- fucking factor now, and in the words of Sweet Brown and her new found fame, "Ain't nobody got time for that!" But instead of being rude, I simply laid the phone down and let him continue to talk while I went on with my day. He'll eventually figure it out, just like I had to...

LIFE ISN'T FAIR 35

AS I paced around my bedroom, I couldn't remember the last time I was this pissed. I had been calling Jermaine all day and I still had not heard back from him. At first my messages were sweet and apologetic. I tried explaining why Steven called and that I think he had finally got the picture. But as the day went on, my calls to Jermaine's cell became more frequent and the voice mail messages became more urgent and now I am spiraling out of control. I haven't been this irrational since Kevin's cheating ass! Just the mere thought of him made me nauseated. As I ran to the downstairs bathroom, I heard Jermaine's truck pull into the driveway. Forgetting the sickening pit in the center of my belly, I turned and ran as fast as I could to the front door. Without stopping to gather my composure, I flung the door open and instead of seeing Jermaine, there stood Kevin...and Shayla's skank ass!

Looking from one to the other, I couldn't hide my disgust and before I knew I was lunging at Shayla's pre-madonna ass! Unable to retreat fast enough, I caught her by that virgin Remy she wore everyday trying to fool everyone like it's hers. In the midst of me throwing a couple of blows and Shayla, I meant Marylyn, flaying her arms letting out a loud screech, Kevin unsuccessfully tried to pull us apart. Then, I felt strong hands on my shoulder from behind me, lift me up off my feet and spun me around like a paper airplane," Nikki, what the hell is wrong with you?" Jermaine's voice rang out!

My chest heaving up and down, I couldn't get anything out. All I could do was just stare at my so- called best friend, and as my baby- daddy stepped closer to defend her, I lunged at her trifling ass again. Unsuccessful this time because Jermaine threw me across his shoulders and carried me upstairs. "Put me down and get that bitch out of my fucking house!" I yelled over my shoulders.

When we reached my bedroom door, my arms were flaying wildly trying to make Jermaine put me down, he then threw me on my double pillow top mattress and straddled me, "What the fuck is wrong with you?" Angrily I just rolled my eyes and turned my head, hoping he could not see the tears sprang to life. Then from the top of the stairs I could hear Chelsea crying and screaming at the top of her lungs, "Get out! You heard my mama, get out my fucking house!"

Jermaine released me and hurried to Chelsea's side, comforting her. I could hear Shayla's ass, in pure Marylyn fashion, "I- I- I'm Sorry," she sobbed, just before the door closed.

Trying to comfort our daughter, I heard Jermaine tell Chelsea," Mommy's okay honey, her and Auntie Shayla were just playing." Just as he was finishing his sentence, I heard him shout, " Hold up, Chelsea!" Then I heard the pitter-patter of little feet heading down the hall and into my bedroom. As bad as I felt right now, seeing her little face was just what I needed. She scurried onto the king-sized bed and into my waiting arms before her dad could catch her. By the time he made it to the door, she was pounding me with tiny, little kisses all over my face. All I could do was giggle uncontrollably. Yes, this was worth fighting for! And as my eyes met those looking cautiously at me from the doorway, I knew I had a lot of explaining to do but this time I am ready to fight for what's mine.

"You have got to be fucking kidding me!" Jermaine said as he paced back and forth in front of our marbel encrusted, California King size bed. "You mean to tell me, you wake up to me every fucking morning and lay down with me every fucking night and you could never find the time to tell me that my daughter might be snatched away from me?" With a sarcastic laugh, he took one last look at me with a face etched in disgust and marched out of the room and probably out of my life. As I heard the front door slam, I could hear him say with even more force from outside the door, "You got to be fucking kidding me!"

Sitting at the foot of Chelsea's bed with my face buried in a towel to muffle my sobs, all I could think about is how empty my life was before Jermaine's call that day. Now, in retrospect, meeting him at Pappadeaux that day was the best and the worst thing that I have ever did. Finally laying eyes on my child was an indescribable joy but the thought of losing her again is a pain one hundred times worse than giving her up the first time. I don't know what I ever did in life to make God hate me so bad, but its obvious that he does. Looking at my sweet, innocent Chelsea lying here without a care in the world, oblivious to the utter turmoil existing in her world. The thought of grabbing her and just running away to where no one could find us kept creeping into my mind...and if I didn't love Jermaine so much I would. Even though the look in his eyes said that it was clearly over between us, the mere thought of bringing him any more pain was simply unbearable. So for now, all I can do is cry and etch every single line of my daughter's beautiful face into my memory forever.

Awakened suddenly, I felt Jermaine's strong arms lift me from floor next to Chelsea's bed and carry me into our bedroom. His masculine scent invaded my nostrils as I nestled closer, "He came back to me," I thought... Or was I dreaming? Before I could open my mouth to speak, he left the room. For the rest of the night, I starred anxiously at the door, hoping and praying that he would come back, take me in his arms and make slow, sweet, passionate love to me. But he never did and as the glowing morning sun made its entryway into my bedroom, I heard my mama's voice saying, "Chile, what don't kill you, will only make you stronger." And I knew then it was over.

Maya answered the phone on the first ring," Bitch, why haven't you been answering my calls? I have been calling you for two damn days and left you a million fucking messages! What the hell..."

Cutting her off, I could barely utter the words, "They're gone!" Then tears erupted from a place deep within and filled the airways. As hard as I tried, I could not get another word out, so I finally just hung up. About thirty minutes later, I heard my door burst open and heard Maya yell out my name. My girl. Following the sounds of my wounded cry, she found me huddled in the middle of Chelsea's bed curled in a fetal position, hugging her pillow close. Not saying a word, she just climbed in the bed next to me, wrapped me in her arms, and rocked me back and forth like a newborn baby. The more I cried, the more she cried. My girl.

I can't be sure how long Maya and I stayed in this position, hell I didn't even know it had been four whole days since Jermaine and Chelsea had left. He told Chesea they were going to visit Mama Joyce for a few days but inside, I knew better. And from the look in her eyes, I believe Chelsea did too. From that moment on, time had no relevance to me. Everything was irrelevant to me. I just wanted to crawl up in a hole and die. "Nikki baby, I know you're hurting but you got to eat something or you'll get sick." I just shook my head from side to side. This time more forcefully, " Oh, yes you are going to eat something if I got to feed it to you my damn self." With that, she jumped her little ass up and laid my head down carefully on the pillow I had squeezed the life out of. Heading downstairs I heard her yell, "I know you got something to eat with your ole' Martha Stewart ass."

Just the mere mention of Martha Stewart just made me burst into yet another round tears. I never thought I would ever miss cooking and cleaning but these last few months, taking care of Jermaine and Chelsea has been the happiest times of my life. I finally had a family in every sense of the word, and now...

UNEXPECTED 36

"NIKKI, snap out of it!" I heard Maya yell. Coming to, I could see tears pooled in the corner of Maya's eyes. Looking around the room hazily, I had no idea what was going on, all I knew was that my head was pounding and dizziness was slowly regaining control over my subconscious once again.

This time it wasn't Maya's voice I heard awakening me from my horrid dream of Shayla and Kevin playing in the park with Chelsea. No, this time I heard the voice that caused me all too many sleepless nights in my life..."Mama...where did you come from? I asked groggily, still unable to open my eyes fully.

Standing near the dresser, with her hands propped on her ample hips, she gave me a look that would send chills down the spine of Satan himself. But instead of being frightened of her like I have been all my life, I rolled over and began to wallow in my self-pity all over again. Not all the mean mug stares mama dearest could muster up could make me feel worse than I do right now. Damn her and her stares, I thought, I got much bigger problems.

My nights were slowly bleeding into my days; as I could no longer tell one from the other and with my black out curtains, the sunlight never came in revealing the earth's secrets. Every hour, on the hour, mama dearest brought her meddling ass into my bedroom trying to get me to get up and eat, or get up and talk, or get up and take a shower but all I felt like doing was rolling over and dying. Without Jermaine, without Chelsea, I didn't have anything else to live for. And for the life of me, I couldn't figure out why Mama and Maya wouldn't take their behinds on home and let me the hell alone. Damn, it wasn't like I was going to put a noose around my neck or anything, I just needed some space to come to terms with my fucked up life without Charlie and the fucking nut factory watching my every single move.

Finally, after a couple of weeks or so of me being closed up in my bedroom, crying constantly, not eating and not sleeping; that sweet, timid lady that had been impersonating my mama must've finally had enough cause the real Mama Dearest burst in my room in a way only she could do..."Got Damnit! I done had bout enough of this shit!" Snatching the covers from over my head and off my body. "Get up, get up right nie! I'm sick and tired of you walking round here like that's the only damn dick on this earth! It might be good but it can't be that damn good!" Pulling me to my feet, with my eyes now stretched wide open, she looked me dead in the eyes and said, "Now, you listen to me girlie...Sometimes, no matter what we do or how good we do it, life just ain't fucking fair and you just can't keep sitting here feeling sorry for yourself. You got to get off your ass and crawl out the hole you in and choose to go on. That's right, I said you got to choose to go on! You got too much to live for! You got one baby that is probably sitting around waiting on you to come looking for her and then you got another one on the way that you probably been too stupid to even realize you're carrying, cause all you thinking about is your damn self!"

Finally finding my voice, I stammered, "Wh-wha-what are you talking bout?"

Shaking her head, "Just like I figured, "You don't even have a clue. Nikki, your ass is just as pregnant as the day is long! I spect in bout seven months you gonna be changing diapers and whipping snot."

Stunned, I couldn't believe my ears, what the hell is this crazy woman talking about now. Who in the hell just sit around and come up with this crazy shit just right out the blue. She always said she has some kind of six senses, I just think she ain't got a lick of sense if you ask me. Pregnant. Yeah right.

Driving down Piedmont, heading to the Fish Market in Buckhead, I looked over at Mama Dearest and wondered to myself, is this woman superhuman or what? My mind and my stomach was literally doing cartwheels for real, while Madame Cleo was sitting over there pumping her hands in the air, looking out the window rapping to the old joint she had blasting from my stereo speakers. "Really Ma?" I thought. She was tickled pink with herself and TI's old hit. Every time the part came on "*I see you over there wit a ass so phat, now why you wanna go and do dat?*" she'd look over and point her finger at me and burst into laughter.

I'm pregnant. Dr. Taylor, my OBGYN, had just confirmed what the six positive EPT test had already alluded to...I'm having a baby and my mama is a fucking psychic! As soon as the doctor told us the results of the blood test, mama dearest jumped up and started praising God! I heard more Hallelujahs and thank you Jesus' than I had ever heard from her in my whole life. As a matter of fact, I can count the number of times I've actually seen her ass in a church but had the nerve to be up in there damn near speaking in tongues. I could see the look of delight and respect beaming from Dr. Taylor and his nurse practitioner, Mack. She had really fooled their ass; the woman who they thought was a fucking mother Theresa reincarnate was more like the bride of Chucky, on steroids! If only they knew, I thought as we strolled out the office with everyone offering HER their well wishes. Hell, I ought to record her ass over here rapping like she sixteen and snap chat that back to their asses and I wonder what they'll think of dear, old, mother dear then. Laughing to myself, looking at her antics, her eyes closed and all...this woman can get a check! Hell, even Cookie Lions off Empire, ain't got shit on my mama!

For the umpteenth time, I dialed Jermaine's cell number, but just like all the times before, I was sent straight to voicemail. With tears in my eyes and sadness in my heart, I refused to leave another message begging him to call me back. Trying to hold onto the little dignity that I had left, I simply hung up the phone.

Lying across the bed, I closed my eyes to stop the submerge of oncoming tears. As I ran my hand across my belly, which was slowly protruding, all I could think about was my baby growing up without knowing his father and me never seeing Chelsea again, then all hell broke loose inside my heart and mama dearest came flooding out! Picking my phone back up, I hit redial on the touch screen, and when that irritating voice mail beep came on this time, I gave that bastard a piece of my mind. "How dare you say you love me, then leave me? How dare you say you love me, and you keep my baby away from me! How dare you do this to me, how dare you!" I sobbed into the phone. "Damn you, Jermaine! Damn, You!"

Slamming the phone down, I cried harder than I'd ever cried in my life. Tears streamed down my face in heavy streams and all I could think is, boy, how I wish mother dearest was still here with me but she had left a month ago, once my second trimester was over and I was no longer wallowing in my misery and hurling it up at the same time. And although she calls ten times a day, it's just not the same. I miss her so much. The last few months have been some of the worst in my life but I can honestly say that I did not have to go through it alone because my mama was there every step of the way. Never in a million years would I have guessed we would be this close but my mama is literally my ride or die chick and without her I don't think I would have made it.

It's funny but I remember it like it was yesterday, how my mama handled my first broken heart. I was thirteen years old and had the biggest crush on Malcolm James, the finest boy in junior high. Malcolm and me had been going together for almost three months and in our teenage world that was a lifetime. One Saturday night Shayla and I begged our parents to let us go to the local skating rink, where everybody, except for us, hung out every weekend. Well of course, mama dearest wasn't having it but Shayla convinced Mr. D to call and advocate on my behalf. Needless to say, Mr. D. always did have a way with words, so after making me wash them stinky ass curly kits for her clients all damn day, she finally told me I can take my fass ass on. I couldn't believe it! She just kept saying, "Take your fass ass on…but you go looking for trouble, you gon find it!" Like always, I didn't know what the hell she was babbling about and I damn sure wasn't trying to figure it out! I was trying to get the hell out of dodge before her bi-polar ass changed her mind. I begged Mr.D. to come get me so I can get dressed at their house. Then it took Shayla damn near two more hours to get my Salt-N-Pepa, high-low bob just right! I was so excited when I looked in the mirror and saw my new look, even though I knew mother dearest was gonna kill me dead for cutting my hair off, seeing the look on Malcolm's face when he saw me was going to be well worth that ass whooping I knew I had coming! When Mr. D. dropped us off at the skating ring, we were so excited we couldn't hide it if we wanted to. Cheesing from ear to ear, we sashayed up to the front entrance. Noticing LaKeshia Littmore, the class tramp, and some of her little flunkies rolling their eyes at us made us even more excited about what the night would bring. All eyes were on us and we knew we were the shit. The sound of Rob Base was exploding in our ears as we made our way into the dark skating area. Girls in crop tops and booty shorts were everywhere and the guys were all over them like flies on shit…and so was Malcolm! As we approached the locker area, I saw Malcolm pull LaTisha, LaKeshia's older sister into a soft embrace, and then he kissed her slowly at first and then more hungrily. What was probably a three second kiss seemed to last three lifetimes for me. My heart was crushed but before I could burst into tears making a pure fool of myself, Shayla quickly pulled me into the bathroom, then into an empty stall. "Stop, that! Bitch, you better not cry!" she scolded. "Fuck that nigga and the ho he with! You better than that anyway!" After about five minutes of Shayla helping me to compose myself, we emerged from the bathroom, into the waiting eyes of LaKeshia and her flunkies, giggling and laughing hysterically. "Just keep laughing, even if it kills you" Shayla whispered in my ear. I did, then she burst into an all out laughing attack in full Marylyn mode, which made me laugh for real, despite the emptiness I was feeling inside. The next thing we knew, the "wish they were fresh crew" were hurling insults at our backs as we walked away. My mama used to always say, misery loves company and when they saw that I wasn't miserable, they couldn't stand it. And just like that, my girl Shayla had helped me to take the power away from their miserable asses. Damn, I miss Shayla.

SOLE CUSTODY 37

THE sudden ring on my doorbell caused me to knock over the glass of warm milk I was nursing. Knowing full well it could only be Maya at my door this time of the night, I took my own sweet time getting to the door. Waddling down the stairs at this point of my pregnancy was a greater task than even I was up to at the moment so whatever Maya was up to better be damn good I thought as I finally reached the bottom step. Once again the incessant ring of the doorbell flooded the room…"Damn, Hold On, I'm coming!" I screamed at the door. Snatching the door open with a vengeance, "Bitch, what the fu--------" Stopping dead in my tracks, I could not believe what I saw, starring back at me were the amber hews of the café' latte eyes that I'd seen every night in my sleep for the last six months. After what seemed like an eternity, I finally managed to let sound escape my now parched throat. "Jer-Jermaine, wha-what are you doing here?"

Clearing his throat, "May I come in? He asked. Clenching my robe tighter, I stepped back casually to allow him entrance into what was once our happy home but now seemed more like a sterile prison lockup. As he stepped over the threshold his gaze lingered on my engorged belly and for a brief moment, I thought I saw something that resembled joy in his rich amber glow but just like a brewing storm, they suddenly turned from a soft, rich amber to deep, murky hue. His jaw line tightened and a stern frown adorned his beautiful face.

He hates me, I thought,

Following him over to the kitchen counter, I reluctantly sat across from him after he didn't even bother to pull out a stool for me, like he'd done so many times before. I guess chivalry really is dead, I thought. For the first time, I noticed the large manila folder he had in his hands. Watching his lips move, I did not hear a single word that was coming out of his mouth. How can he just sit across this counter from me, the counter that we made love on for the very first time, and act like I wasn't shit to him? Hearing Chelsea's name, I snapped out of the trance I was in, "How is she?" I asked, tears instantly springing to my eyes.

"She's fine" was all he offered and went back into his monologue. Before I let the waterworks explode, I heard my mama's voice inside my head, "Never give a bitch the satisfaction of knowing you care." Sitting straight faced, starring him directly in the eye, I listened intently as he explained his legal disposition to me and told me how my testimony was going to be influential in the custody battle with Kevin. His custody battle. After he finished, I sat quietly, taking in all the information and quickly deciphering it in my head. Slowly, I nodded my head. Getting up from the counter, he came around like he was about to help me to my feet but after taking another quizzical glance at my protruding stomach; he made a quick turn and headed towards the front door. My hurt stopped. After finally getting to my feet, on my own I might add, I followed him to the front door contemplating everything I had just heard and everything that had transpired since he walked in the door. As he opened the door and stepped out, he turned to me and asked, "Do you have any questions?"

Looking him dead in the eyes, like I seen my mama doing people my whole life, I said, "No, I'm all clear."

Before he could get "Good," out of his mouth good, I said, "I'm clear, that you must think I'm a damn fool if you think I'm stupid enough to help you take my baby away from me! Not once did you mention any joint custody arrangement for you and I. You think I don't realize that you getting full custody from Kevin don't mean that you're also getting full custody from me too? You must be out your rabbit ass mind! Fuck Kevin and fuck you too!" I screamed before slamming the door.

"You already did!" He yelled through the closed door and now my heart literally felt like it was falling out of my chest. I slumped down to the floor and cried my heart out. With sleep reluctantly unwelcoming me, hour by hour, my heart became heavier and heavier as I laid on the floor in the fetal position, drowning in tears, snot and piss, crying for my beautiful child that I haven't seen or spoke to in six months, my unborn child, who was not going to get a chance to know his father and for the misery that I now called me life.

Suddenly a clenching pain took over the lower part of my abdomen causing me to scream out in excruciating pain. Trying to pull myself up from the wet heap on the floor, I could not move and the pain took over my body again causing more tears to run down my face in a flowing stream. Looking down at my now aching belly, I saw pools and pools of dark crimson covering my cloths and soaking into my plush carpet. "Oh, my God!" I yelled, my own voice chilling me down deep to my core, "My Baby," I cried before the red turned into black and my consciousness faded out.

SECOND CHANCE 38

FADING in and out of consciousness, I could hear someone say, "She's lost too much blood, we got to take this baby now or we're going to loose them both! Nooooooo, I was screaming inside of my head but I could not get my mouth to move. Please Lord, I thought, please help me open my eyes. Save my baby, please save my baby, I thought. I can die but please save my ba--------!

Feeling a slight pressure in my head, I painfully batted my eyelids, the incoming light sending the pain already taking residency inside my head into sudden shock. "Nikki, Nikki, can you hear me?" I heard Maya's voice invade my eardrums.

"Oh My God, Nikki," I heard my mama say, "Oh, thank you Jesus!" she exclaimed! Not able to focus my eyes, I'm suddenly not so sure if that's my mama voice I hear after all. If it is, I must be dead I thought cause my mama don't know Jesus...she needs Jesus!

I heard Shayla yell, "It's a miracle!" in full Marylyn mode.

"Wh-what happened, Wh-where am I" I stammered as I felt a cold glass press gently against my lips. The water coated my parched throat feeling like liquid velvet.

"Sweetheart, said my mother, Don't try to speak. You're in the hospital."

Suddenly I remembered the clenching pain that I'd felt that night... "My baby?" I asked and the room suddenly went quiet and dark at the same time. Please God no, not my baby I thought as my subconscious drifted into oblivion once again.

This time when I opened my eyes, the room was very quite. As my eyes began to focus, I saw my mama and daddy stretched out on a reclining chair over in the far corner, Maya was sitting on Shayla's lap in a chair to the right of my parents and as I looked around the room...there they were. Those eyes. Pools of soft amber gold was starring intently back at me. No words were uttered, no gestures were made; we simply gazed at one another like we would never see each other again. Damn, I love that man. Then sleep took over me once again.

I was unsure of how long I'd been in the hospital and even more unsure of how I'd gotten here but somebody was going to tell me what happened to my baby, I thought as I willed myself to finally regain complete consciousness. All I could remember was looking down and seeing blood and hearing someone say we've got to take the baby. "My Baby," I screamed, startling everyone in the room. "Where's my baby?" The hospital heart monitor I was hooked to started beeping loudly as my mama, Maya and Shayla, rushed to my side trying to calm me down. Crying hysterically, I began yanking at the IV in my arm trying to get out the hospital bed. "Please, tell me what happened to my baby!" Suddenly, Jermaine ran back into the room and like Jesus splitting the red sea, he was at my side.

"Shhh-Shhh," he said, as he rubbed my face, "calm down sweetheart, he's going to be okay, our baby boy is going to be okay." Looking into his eyes, I saw warmth, I saw love and I saw my future.

As I lay awake in bed, anxious to get the day started, I looked over at the wonderful man whom I was getting ready to share the rest of my life with. With her feet and arms dangling over both her father, and me, Chelsea was gritting her teeth as she slept peacefully. Also, snuggled up against me, looking up with the glossiest amber eyes, just like his father's, was my beautiful baby boy, Chance.

After two months in the hospital's NICU, our little prizefighter was finally able to come home. Born three months early, Chance graced the world at 1 pound, 3 ounces on my living room floor. When I was finally out of the woods, I learned that the night I went into labor, Jermaine was outside my front door. According to him, once I slammed the door in his face and he hurled the insult at me, he turned to march away but then he heard my despair as I sank to my floor in tears. He said something in his heart would not let him leave me like that, so he sank outside the front door trying to conceal the pain he was in, finally crying himself to sleep. He said a startling shrill that rocked him to the core awakening him, shortly before dawn. At first he said he thought I was just being emotional again but when he heard my second scream he knew something was wrong. Forgetting he still had his house key, he began banging on the door but when I never responded, he kicked my door down and found me passed out on the floor covered in blood.

Dialing 9-1-1, he reported a possible miscarriage, telling the operator that I appeared to be around three or four months pregnant. By the time the paramedics made it to my place, Jermaine had managed to elevate my feet and was sponging my body down with a wet dishcloth trying to decrease the fever he felt radiating from my body. After quickly examining me, the paramedics told Jermaine that his wife wasn't going to make it to the hospital that they had to take the baby now or risk loosing us both. 'Save them, save them both he yelled at the paramedics, as they prepared to deliver a baby he knew belonged to another man, probably Kevin, which in his mind explained my reluctance to help him with his custody battle for Chelsea. Never having been so afraid in his life, Jermaine held my head in his lap as the two veteran paramedics performed an emergency cesarean on my living room floor, bringing my little man into this world.

According to my mother, when Jermaine called her and my dad, he was hysterical, saying he had a car on the way to get them, demanding they get to Northside hospital as soon as possible. He then proceeded to call, Maya and Shayla and told them what had happened and urged then to please come quickly. My blood pressure had elevated so high that I had a light stroke during delivery and ended up going in and out of consciousness for days. Chance was rushed to the hospital's NICU, where he was placed in an incubator to raise his body temperature; a breathing tube was inserted to help him breathe because his lungs were not fully developed. We were both in critical condition but Jermaine never once left our side. As I looked over at him, I just thank God that he was there that frightful night...I hate to think about what would have happened if he wasn't!

My little man was already two weeks old before I was able to see him for the very fist time. As soon as Jermaine wheeled me into the NICU, my eyes was instantly drawn to his incubator, even from across the room, I knew exactly which one of those babies was mine. I began to cry as I starred at him through the incubator, hooked up to all those tubes. Then I looked at his nametag and saw it read, "Chance" in bold, bright letters. I guess Jermaine followed my gaze and said, "I hope you don't mind, but I didn't want him in this world without a name, so I took the liberty. But we can change it if you like."

"No, no...I love it and to be honest, I had no idea what to name him. Looking up at him, I asked, "So, how did you come up with "Chance"?"

Looking down at the floor, he seemed to be nervous. Then he said, " Well, that night when I came over, I came over to beg you to forgive me and to take me back because I'd finally talked to Shayla and she explained everything to me. That night when I left, after I had to keep you from killing your best friend, It wasn't just the fact that you had not told me that Kevin was Chelsea's biological father but also because I felt like you must have still been in love with him for you to behave so angrily towards Shayla. But, after months and months of me avoiding calls from you, your mom, Shayla and Maya, Shayla finally showed up at my mom's early one morning and was waiting at my truck when I left for work.

"You mean, Shayla came to New Orleans?"

"Yessssssss, and in pure Marylyn mode might I add," we both laughed. She told me how angry you were when Kevin showed up at Jason's parents' and how you vowed he would not break up your family or take Chelsea away from us. She was actually the one that provided me with the evidence I needed to fight Kevin in the custody battle."

"Really?"

"Yup," nodding his head with tears still glistening in his eyes. "Nikki, you've got to know she loves you and Chelsea more than anyone in the world. She felt like this whole fiasco was her fault because she was the one that posted the pictures on her Facebook page. She was willing to do what ever it took to keep Kevin from taking Chelsea away from us; even if that meant losing you."

Tears exploded down my face as I thought about my dear friend and how much I'd missed her. Jermaine continued, "Because of Shayla, we got all types of proof of different illegal activities Kevin has been involved with over the years. So much, in fact, if it ever came to light, the league would have no other choice than to ban him for life, with no hesitation. Especially with all the negative publicity they've been rocked with lately. But not just that, your girl was also able to get close enough to him to find out that he had known for years that you had been pregnant from him and had possibly had a miscarriage or given the baby up for adoption. But at the time, he was so self-absorbed that he did not care to be a father, so he ignored it. And according to Shayla, who is now in law school following in her dad's footsteps, Kevin's failure to exercise his paternal rights the moment he found out years ago, the judge will not look at his custody petition favorably. So, even though you said "fuck me" on you last voice mail two months ago, I was determined to make you understand and take me back but when you opened the door and I saw your baby budge, my heart was crushed. You looked as if you were only about three or four months along, so I just assumed you had gone back to that asshole, after all, the nigga still had his own ringtone and shit. Or, I thought maybe you and Kevin had resolved your unfinished business, especially when you refused to help me fight him for custody. So, at that point, I just wanted to hurt you, like you'd hurt me but when I heard you crying like that, I just couldn't take it. I couldn't leave you like that. Then, when you awakened me with your screams of agony and I burst in seeing you lying in a pool of blood, I thought I'd lost you forever. I didn't care whose baby it was, I just wanted you both to be okay. Everything was so hectic that night; you were critical, he was critical; all I could do was pray. It was two whole days before they finally allowed me inside the NICU to see the baby, and as soon as I looked at him, my heart melted but when he looked up at me with those rich, amber eyes, I knew I had a second "Chance…"

Still Got Joy

EPILOGUE

"MARILYN! I mean, Shayla," Maya said, "Will you please stop making this about you, nobody gives a fuck how you look today, you're not the fucking bride!" These two had been going at it all damn day. I felt plum sorry for the poor make-up artists who have spent most of their day refereeing theses two heifers rather than actually doing any make-up or hair. Jade, the owner of Kiss-N-Makeup and Jason's younger sister, ever the professional, knew this would be the case with these two, so she had sent out her entire glam squad to cover my wedding.

When Jade opened my dressing room door, where she and I had been held up for hours; I stepped out into the larger dressing room and a daunting hush immediately fell over my beautiful bridesmaids. Surprisingly, even my maid and matron of honor were speechless. Then, I looked over and saw tears sprang to life in the eyes of my mother and Chelsea. Fighting the urge to breakdown, I said, "No, not even happy tears today! Not yet anyway!" We all laughed. My heart was so filled with love.

Just then we heard a quiet knock at the door, "Sweetheart," Mr. D. said, "Someone is here, he wants to speak to you for a moment."

Everyone yelled, "Noooooooooo!" " It's bad luck!"

Mr. D. stuck his head in the door, "Give me some credit, Ladies, don't you think I already know that! It's not Jermaine." He moved aside and Kevin stepped from around him. Looking ultra sexy, standing there in his cream colored, double breasted tuxedo, with a gold and tangerine tie and handkerchief was my first love, my daughter's father and...my groom's best man.

"You look beautiful, Nikki." Then his eyes fell upon Chelsea. "Look at my gorgeous little Princess!"

She waltzed over, just like she'd seen Shayla do on numerous occasions and hugged him tightly, "Thank you, God Father. You look han-som too," she giggled, it was so adorable.

Kevin stood and walked over to me, looking me in my eyes, he said, "Nik, I know it's late but I have never said the words to you that I should have said a long time ago. I am so sorry for hurting you all those years ago. I was young, stupid and immature. What you had to go through, I wouldn't wish on my worst enemy and you certainly did not deserve any of it. You were perfect then and you are perfect now. I can never express how grateful I am to you and Jermaine for allowing me a place in your lives and Chelsea's life. I wish you both the best, that's all I have ever wanted for you. Will you accept my apology?"

Taken completely by surprise at Kevin's apology, I slowly nodded my head and kissed him on the cheek. After our first rocky encounter on Father's Day and his subsequent visit to our Alpharetta home at Jermaine's insistence a couple of days later, things between Kevin and I had been quite volatile. After my release from the hospital and after Jermaine revealed to him all the evidence my girl Shayla, had on him, Kevin quickly agreed to the terms Jermaine and I had established. After that, the three of us told Chelsea he was her biological father. Being the bright child she has always been, she immediately began calling Kevin, God Father, which seemed to please him; as well as, Jermaine and I. From that moment on, he became part of our family. Over time, we have developed a genuine friendship and he and Jermaine are closer than ever before.

As I stood on the outside of the chapel doors, with my sweetheart neckline, diamond encrusted, cinched waist, one of a kind, Vera Wang gown, awaiting the surprise tune that Jermaine had chosen to fill the chapel's airways as I walked down the aisle, my stomach turned in knots. Suddenly, my father turned to me and nervously said, "I know I wasn't half the dad that you wanted me to be, and none of what you deserved. But I want you to know that it was not because I didn't want to be...I just didn't know how to be. You have and always will be the joy of my life and I am so proud of the woman you've become." The tears finally fell, it seems I'd been waiting all my life to hear THOSE words from THAT man!

Retrieving an old handkerchief from his pockets, he wiped my tears and said "Hush, Baby, you're too beautiful to cry. You see this here, this old handkerchief; this is the only thing my parents ever gave me. My grandma said my mama took it from my pops and wiped her tears with it and laid it next to me on the bed, as they walked out the door to start a new life in Chicago, leaving me behind with the promise to come back for me, but they never did. This is all I've ever had of theirs, but I want you to have it." He then wiped another fresh tear, careful not to smear my make-up, then folded the handkerchief and tucked it carefully into my bouquet. I learned more about my daddy in those three minutes that I had my entire life.

As the music began, the doors opened. The sultry voice of Freddie Jackson filled the chapel, *"You are my lady. You're everything I need and more..."* and an electric force greater than anything I've ever felt in the world, moved my feet fluidly down the aisle to the man I plan on spending the rest of my life with, My Sexy Chocolate. Jermaine stood tall, his eyes never leaving mine as I made my way gracefully down the aisle, with my father's aide. As I joined him at the altar, our hearts smiled and our souls united forever.

J'Sat Necolle

Still Got Joy

ABOUT THE AUTHOR

A native of Soperton, GA, mother of one, and soon-to-be grandmother of a beautiful baby girl, this is J'sat Necolle 's debut novel. A late bloomer, she earned a Bachelor of Business Administration Degree from Augusta State University in 2006, followed by a Masters of Business Administration Degree in 2010, then opened a successful retail bakery in Atlanta, GA. in 2011. Here she allows her creative talents to flourish in the wonderment of cake artistry.

J'Sat Necolle has always believed that when GOD blesses you with a talent, HE wants you to use it. Now that she has successfully followed one dream, she is now turning her passions back to her first loves, reading and writing.

J'Sat Necolle has always had a passion for love and romance. When it comes to writing, J'Sat seeks to inspire others to believe that real love does still exit. A proud advocate of empowerment, J'Sat's remarkable creativity and social awareness allows her to bring many characters, subjects and genres to life on her pages. So, stay tuned to be inspired to love again. For more information on this author visit www.anaproductions.org

For The Love of Keria